Gringo & Greaser

Gringo & Greaser

By

HUGH R. MORRIS

Copyright © 2003 by Hugh Morris.
Printed in the United States. All rights reserved.

ISBN: 1-58597-184-7

Library of Congress Control Number: 2003104568

A division of Squire Publishers, Inc.
4500 College Blvd.
Leawood, KS 66211
1/888/888-7696
www.leatherspublishing.com

Dedicated to

Dee Meriwether Morris

Wife of 52 years

and

My support group

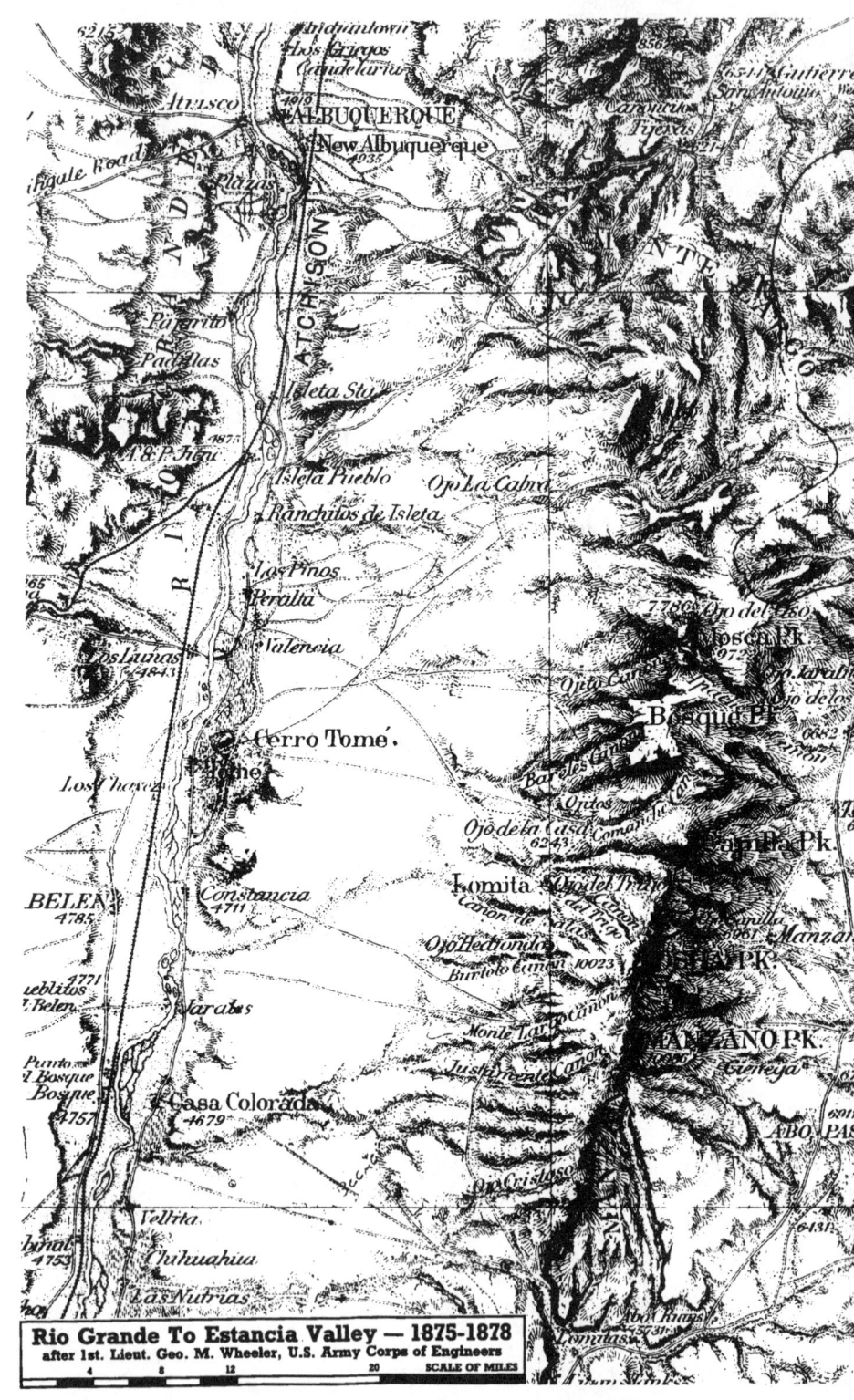

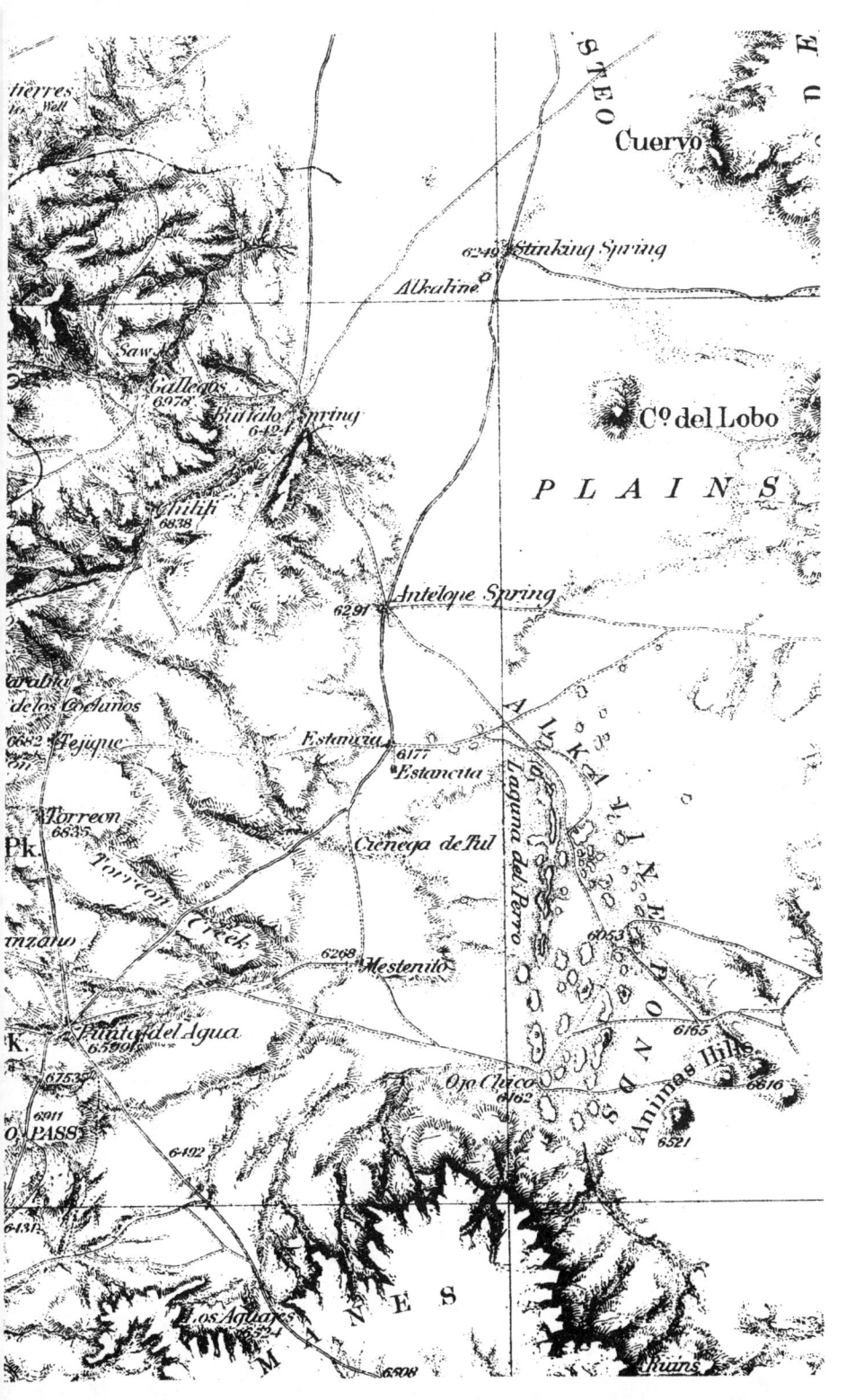

CHAPTER 1

MERCILESS AFTERNOON SUN burned through Martín Wolf's coarse cotton shirt. Squirming in it relieved the itching — a bit. Out of habit, but more from affection he reached out and scratched the neck of his slate-gray gelding, Pizarra, named after the color of the stone. The horse tested newly shod hooves by pawing gravel on the dusty, rutted road, then snorted loudly, impatient to move on.

As he fingered drops of sweat off the end of his hooked nose, through parched lips Martín said, *"Por Dios,* it's hot!"

No relief came from looking down at the farrier framed in waves of heat from the forge behind him. Justino Abeyta, without question the best in the Estancia Valley for horseshoeing and other blacksmithing needs, placed his hand on Pizarra's flank and looked up at the tall horseman.

"Que Caballo! Martín. *Un de million.* Your father must have been *loco* to geld him."

With a look of half pride, half smile, he answered, "So no colts. Hey, Justino, I was only 14 when my father gave me Pizarra. What could I do? *Un caballo regalado* — you know what they say about gift horses."

Leaning back in the deep Mexican saddle, he dug two silver dollars out of his rough cotton pants. Pizarra, topping sixteen hands, twisted his neck around to nip the farrier touching him. Martín jerked on the reins.

"He may not be grateful, but I am," and smiled as he

dropped the coins into the pocket of Justino's oft-mended leather apron.

Cash, especially American silver dollars, was in short supply in the valley. To show his appreciation, Abeyta exposed a mouthful of bad teeth.

Almost by habit, Justino's eyes searched Martín's face. Most Mexicans did and he knew why — curious that his dark skin contrasted so sharply with his blue Anglo eyes. Used to the scrutiny, he wondered why he should be accountable for having mixed parentage, Mexican and Anglo-American. Could one culture be better than combining two?

"Back to Manzano?" asked Justino.

"Not straightway. I'm taking another look at Quarai Mission. Don't know why that ruin fascinates me so."

"Well, give my regards to your father."

Considering his current relationship with his father, he rather doubted if he would. With a friendly nod to Justino, he touched Pizarra into a brisk walk. Surprised by his abrupt departure, Justino fumbled for words of warning to shout to the disappearing rider. He had suspicions about what might be going on at Quarai and would sound foolish if he just blurted them out. Now it was too late.

And Abeyta had good reason to form suspicions about Quarai, the ruins of a large 17th century church and mission, one of three built in the area by the Franciscans. The mission was just a mile from his house, a small adobe in the barely populated hamlet of Punta del Agua. It fronted on the only road through the village. Anything that moved, north or south, had to pass his house. Valley men, their wives and children, out-of-valley strangers, driven stock, spring wagons and solid wheel *carretas,* all drifted through town toward whatever their destination. Widowed and lonely, Abeyta hungered to talk to anyone passing through. During the day he would sometimes follow strangers for a snatch of conversation, a smile, or even just a nod.

But not at night.

Cattle rustling in the Estancia Valley had a long tradition, was almost endemic there, and made easier by the common and lazy practice of letting cattle loose to forage on their own. Periodically awakened at night by the sound of stock being driven by his house, Justino stayed behind his locked door but was curious enough to look for sign next morning. Tracks and droppings from these nocturnal drives always led west to the remnants of the old church and mission, Quarai. What then happened to the stock Justino didn't know nor care to find out. To him, these late night drives seemed larger and more purposeful than the casual cattle thefts he was used to hearing about

Too late now to tell Martín about what he knew and what he suspected. His friend was nearly out of sight. Angry at his silence, regretting it, with his ragged boot he toed meaningless lines in the dirt. Why was he tongue-tied with a friend who might be harmed by his silence?

Martín looked back with affection at the diminishing figure of Justino Abeyta standing in the middle of the road. Close to sixty, Abeyta had been a friend as long as he could remember, coming to Punta del Agua with his father to get their horses reshod. Abeyta stayed trim through sparse living and an obsession for hunting. His small house, shop and forge were in the middle of a typical mid-valley village with nondescript stone and adobe homes. Despite the isolation, his reputation as a creative blacksmith brought him as much work as he could handle.

His concern about what might be going on at Quarai was justified, but its location and former function made it seem an unlikely site to suspect of being involved in cattle rustling. Maybe that was why it would be an ideal location. Soaring walls of the roofless church, "La Señora de la Purissima Concepcion," still stood. Disorderly piles of rubble outlined the location of its former *convento,* Quarai's extensive sleeping and eating quarters, stables, work and storerooms. Conceived by the order of Franciscans more than two hundred and fifty years previously, the old church and mission complex mission had been built on a most unlikely site, the edge of the enormous, dry Estancia Valley, more than two hundred and fifty square miles of virtually unpopulated land. The Franciscans chose the site for good reasons. The nearby Indian pueblo of Quarai solved the brotherhood's two most pressing needs: plenty of almost-slave labor with which to build, and many souls ready for harvesting when the mission was completed. In front of it, flowing half above, half below marshy ground, a sluggish stream finally surfaced as a dependable, year-round spring near Abeyta's village. From the spring came its name Punta del Agua, "point of water."

On the road north from his village was a tier of other small towns: Manzano, Torreon, Tajique, Chilili and Buffalo Spring. Even further north the road led to Tijeras Canyon, a natural corridor running east and west between the northern end of the Manzano Mountains and the southern terminus of the precipitous Sandias. Along this corridor ran the road west to the growing community of Albuquerque.

Before reaching the mission, Martín turned Pizarra up a path to a rise from which he could look down on the walls of the church, the swelling curve of its nave, and the ruins that outlined the mission area. He wondered how Quarai had looked when the mission was populated and functioning. What a majestic and surprising sight it must have been for a visitor to this desolate spot!

Few adobe bricks were used in Quarai's construction. Underlying the whole area was a reef of red sandstone. Slabs of the easily split red rock were mined by Quarai Indians to become the fabric of the church and its convento walls. Two centuries later more pieces of sandstone cemented with adobe mud were used to build many walls of the simple houses in Punta del Agu.

From where he sat his horse, Martín could see east far into the Estancia Valley and west into the canyons, then the mountains beyond the mission. Dismounting, idly scratching Pizarra's nose resting on his shoulder, he looked into the apparently sere valley. Only a native could know how rich its resources really were.

The gelding stretched his neck down to saw off a tuft of grama grass. Abundance of this nutritious feed made the valley area one of the West's richest grazing lands. Also favoring the Estancia Valley were underground natural aquifers carrying badly needed runoff from Manzano Mountain snow more than a dozen miles out to the year-round springs of Antelope, Buffalo and Estancia. Anchored far to the northwest he could just see the conical landmark Cerrito de Lobo appearing to heave in a sea of fierce valley heat. Due east undulated the Perdenal and Animas hills. Erosion from Manzano surface water sculpted alluvial fans that spread like hands into the valley.

He knew each fold like the back of his own hand. From the moment he was old enough to shoot a rifle, Martín had hunted the valley and the forty miles of mountains running north and south behind his home in the town of Manzano. West of town the mountains peaked at over ten thousand feet, a formidable barrier between the Estancia Valley and the Rio Grande.

In the middle of the valley, strung like beads and glinting in the late afternoon sun, were salt ponds collectively called "Laguna del Perro," saline remnants of what had been an enormous lake covering the valley floor millenniums earlier.

With nothing but bad memories from his childhood about these lagoons, he shook his head in disgust. To gather brine from the shrinking ponds from which to make salt, twice yearly he was forced to go out to them with his father and their Manzano neighbors. Slowly, and in long *cordons* they wound their way out onto the valley floor. Caught between the scorching glare from the salt pans and a pitiless sun, the boy quickly became dehydrated from the hard, disagreeable work.

As if the work wasn't enough, each evening he had to listen to his father's tirades about how badly Mexicans were treated by Anglo-Americans. He didn't understand half of what his father raged about, except to wonder why Anglos were so awful. The litany of wrongs was endless: conflicts over land, illegal fencing of communal springs, outright theft of land by political intrigue financed by eastern money, crooked courts, illegal diversion of water from Mexican *acequias,* the widely held opinion that Mexicans were lazy and ignorant, name calling — "greasers" and worse.

An Anglo-American married to a Mexican, Aaron was hyper-sensitive about these issues, all of which had validity. It was a point of view an older Martín might have understood. Uncomfortable, impressionable, confused and too young to make considered judgments, he only half listened to his father. For years he was convinced that the fault must be all Anglo.

Shaking off these memories with a shudder, he turned around to look past the church to the west. Late afternoon sun began to balloon in size as it dropped toward the horizon, also making it appear to hurry in its descent behind the Manzanos. It seemed just minutes until there was left only a sense of the golden glow that had just been. Looking back into the valley, he watched shadows eat their way across the valley, its floor still seeming to writhe from day-long baking.

Effortlessly he remounted and a touch of spurs set Pizarra in motion down toward the mission ruins. The horse stepped warily around scattered stone blocks, all that remained of the foundations and *plazuela* of the old Lucero house built on the knoll centuries after the church was completed. A hundred yards away lay the husk of the Quarai church in ruinous repose, a sight Martín never tired of. Each visit evoked a new vision. Quarai would become a castle, an old fort, whatever his imagination could conjure up.

In the dying light of this early summer evening the church's broken red stone walls glowed like a huge, fresh wound. Anywhere, the church would have been a huge structure. In a countryside dotted only with small adobes, it was immense. Unroofed by an ancient fire, the building had weathered badly. Walls were deeply scalloped where windows or other openings had been. Fortunately, the physical integrity of the sturdy structure was still intact. In places the flanks of its cruciform nave towered over forty feet high. Cut into the tops of the walls were regularly spaced slots for *vigas,* wood beams once bearing the roof, now burned and rotted away. Motionless on his horse, he shared with the early summer evening the church's beauty and shadows on the low tumbled walls outlining the convento.

A flash of light suddenly appeared in a viga slot on top of the wall directly in front of him. He blinked in disbelief. Impossible! This place was deserted. Another flash. His mind thumbed through possibilities. Imagination? A trick of the sun's afterglow? Reflection from a piece of polished stone? A signal! Looking quickly to the east, he saw no answering flash. What light was left came from the west.

Another phenomenon. Not a sound. Birds and insects seemed to have fallen silent. Even the constant breeze. Quickly, silence fled, shattered by the sharp impact of a rock striking the paved floor of the church. Immediately there followed the sound of a cascade of smaller stones. He watched as a bright object, it looked like a bullseye lantern, drop a few feet below the viga slot from which the flash had come. It was quickly retrieved by a lanyard that held it. For what seemed like a lifetime he waited for something else to happen. It did.

He urged his horse a few yards nearer the church. Almost immediately came the crack of a rifle, the bullet impacting at Pizarra's front hooves, spraying them both with a painful fusillade of sandstone chips. Moments later, horses, hidden within the church walls, tore out of its front entrance and west up Cañon Sapato. Unarmed except for the knife always on the back of his belt, a startled Martín wanted no part of whatever was happening. Brutally neck-reining the gray around, he left the mission area at a dead run.

Once well on the road north toward his home in Manzano, he slowed Pizarra to a fast walk. Except for the faintest afterglow beyond the crest of the mountains, night dropped over the two like a cloak. In the near-dark Pizarra's newly shod hooves struck occasional sparks on shards of sandstone they mined from the road. Little more than a well-used path, its edges were roughly defined by thickets of piñon and juniper interspersed with fallen boulders from the steep mountain slope, bare areas of caliche, scattered chamisa bushes and clumps of grama grass.

Moving rhythmically in his saddle to Pizarra's steady pace, Martín wondered what could be possibly happening at Quarai. The people he'd surprised certainly wanted no visitors. Who were they? Used to monitoring sounds in the outdoor world, his sensitive hearing picked up the minute resonance of hoofbeats behind him. He stopped to listen to their muted cadence. Two riders — at least, were apparently trailing him. Moving noiselessly off the road into a depression thick with juniper, he dismounted, covered Pizarra's nose with his hand to quiet him and still the jingling of his curb bit.

"One snort of welcome," he whispered, "and it's all over for you."

Uncertain what had happened to the man they were following, the riders halted almost opposite the juniper grove. Martín peered up into the last of the afterglow which barely outlined the riders. He could see both had rifles in saddle scabbards and a bulge on their hips.

"How could that som bitch jus disappear, Jack?" the rear horseman drawled. " 'N why in hell was he sniffin' roun' the mission anyway? 'Spose he knows what we're doin' there?"

"Shut up, Rafe. You want him to hear you?"

"Did'j'a see the big gray," continued Rafe, ignoring Jack's warning. "Betcha sixteen hands. Betcha he thinks he looks swell forkin' thet big devil. Like to be on it steda this crowbait."

"Forget the gray, Rafe," snapped Jack. "That greaser knows this country a goddam sight better'n we do. Doan know if he saw anything but if'n he did and talks, that hombre could put us out of business."

Texans, Martín said to himself. He'd listened to many. And as often as he had heard the word "greaser," it always irritated him.

The riders moved on north toward Manzano. Not much wiser from what he'd heard, but more wary, he mounted and rode toward town, too. For safety he took a little-used cattle trail paralleling the main road. Except for light from candles and kerosene lanterns glowing dimly through the scraped hide glazing of windows facing the street, the town was dark. Lack of light discouraged the Texans from actively looking for him.

Besides, they had another reason to be in Manzano.

CHAPTER 2

UP MANZANO'S DARK, short main street straight toward home Martín rode. The incident at the mission rattled him badly, like unintended contact with a hive of bees. The shot that missed him. A warning? Or meant to kill? To whom could he talk about it?

Certainly not his father who scorned most things he did. Aaron would probably think he made up the story. What Martín dreaded most about going home was the near certainty of another argument with his father, now a nightly affair. His was a love-hate relationship with Aaron. Hate, because his father's every word was barbed or plainly acrimonious. Hate, because Aaron made it a point to denigrate him no matter what he did. And maybe hate since his father began drinking heavily, sparking increasingly frequent arguments over increasingly trivial matters.

The love, affection perhaps a better word, side of his relationship with his father was based on what Aaron had done for him when he was younger. He owed two debts he could never repay: a love of reading and, for his time and place, a unique education. Thanks to a well-stocked library and Aaron's insistence, he became a compulsive reader in a desert of illiterates. Besides greatly expanding his vocabulary, his view of the world no longer centered on the Estancia Valley. He outgrew home learning rapidly. Schools in the area were few and inferior.

Aaron heard that a priest in Tome, a small town on the edge of the Rio Grande, had started a school premised that there was more to education than Catholic doctrine, standard fare in the few existing New Mexican schools. He made the two-day ride to Tome to meet the man, salty Father Jean Baptiste Ralliere, a worldly and practical priest imported from France.

When they met at the schoolhouse, the cordial Ralliere laughed when Aaron said, "I hear you're doing something different here."

"And as a result, making myself the most unpopular priest in the diocese. Well, it had to be done. Even before I walked into this cracked adobe schoolhouse, I knew there'd be rows of children learning their catechism and passages from the Bible by rote."

"You mean religion hasn't got a place in education?" asked Aaron.

"Of course it has. But there's a lot more to education than the Bible and catechism. Anyway, I was right about what I was going to see in that schoolhouse. The young priest teaching there even waved a stick at his pupils like a maestro with a baton. I suppose he thought rhythm would somehow help their memories. It took me only a week to decide what needed changing, then two months to get up the nerve to do it."

"Change isn't very popular anywhere," said Aaron.

"Traditionalists around here got really angry, even before they knew what I was going to change. At mass one Sunday, with the parents of many of my soon-to-be students sitting before me, I told them what was going to change. Then I said, 'School is the place to prepare your children for life. Here in church we'll help prepare them for life hereafter.' "

"So, what did you change?"

"We kept a few religious subjects and teach spelling, geography, arithmetic and history. We'll take any student as far into those subjects as they'd like to go. Now we've added practical subjects such as blacksmithing, carpentry, animal husbandry, even crop selection. For the girls we've got sewing, cooking and nursing.

"Fathers of some of the students, most of them farmers, also help teach. So do a few of the mothers. They like the changes and feel part of the learning process. But townspeople hate these parents and probably me, too, though they still come to church on Sunday."

Ralliere's refreshing frankness impressed Aaron. What his son, fourteen years old, rebellious, cocky, strong and something of an intellectual snob would think didn't matter. He needed this kind of environment. Ignoring his embarrassment, Aaron rode with Martín to Tome to make certain he got to the school. Once there, any sense of superiority Martín felt over the other students was quickly deflated by boys as tough as he and by the uncompromising Ralliere. When first there, he thought he knew something about almost everything. Quickly he found there was a lot more to learn about most of what he thought he knew. And, surprisingly, discovered there were many things about which he knew almost nothing. Whatever the school and Ralliere himself would teach, Martín soaked up along with a healthy dose of humility.

Could it be seven years since he'd left? Now, reluctantly, he worked for his father who had changed radically. Have I done anything to make him change, Martín wondered? Or is it something I don't know about? There's got to be a reason.

* * * * *

By habit Pizarra turned into their lane. The Wolfs' adobe home was just above the head of a small valley on the west side of Manzano. "U" shaped to enclose a central patio, one wing housed his parents and in the other were rooms for him and his sister. Across the base of the "U" was the *sala,* a dining area and an adjacent but enclosed *cocina.* The entire front of the adobe was covered by a long *portal,* the roof of which overhung a rough puncheon walkway. Centered in the patio, an enormous cottonwood provided a perfect shield from the hot valley sun.

In the dark Pizarra headed unerringly for the stable. Frenzied barking by Felita, a bitch border collie kept for breeding and as a part-time pet, welcomed Martín home. After lighting the stable lantern, he backed Pizarra into his stall, fed and rubbed him down. Felita gave him a glazed look of satisfaction as he scratched behind her ears. After blowing out the lantern, in the dark he carefully skirted the kitchen garden and stepped over the small *acequia* that watered it, one of several ditches of running water fed by a nearby spring. Chicken coops came alive with the squawking of startled hens. He entered the *sala* just as his mother came in from the kitchen at its far end. Despite two children and her healthy appetite, Daisy Wolf was still small and trim. She and her son looked at each other warmly. Both smiled, his a bit forced.

"*Hola!* So there you are. Do you know what time it is? I should have given up holding supper."

Embarrassed, he held both hands out. "I know, I know." Not wanting to worry her, he added, "You'd be bored with the details, but it couldn't be helped."

"Where'd you go today? You disappeared even before I had breakfast. Maybe I got up late."

Both laughed. Nobody got up earlier than tireless Daisy. The smile almost always on her dark Mexican face reflected an inner lightheartedness in sharp contrast to iron-gray hair pulled back into a severe bun.

Martin summoned another grin for her benefit. *"El tiempo perdido no se recobra* (time lost can never be recovered). Honestly, my intentions were good, but everything took longer than I thought it would."

"Then I don't want to hear about it."

"But, Mother, I also did some things for you. Did you notice the feeder *acequia* in your kitchen garden? It's cleared of weeds. And with luck, those traps I set and baited in the arroyo behind the house will get rid of the coyotes taking your chickens."

He added in a prickly voice, "Both stables are clean, but

I'm sure Father didn't look or wouldn't mention it if he did."

At that moment in walked his sister Ofelia carrying a clay *olla* full of water. "The real reason the stable's so clean is that I swept it out two days ago, not you, Martín!"

Tall for a woman, yet a head shorter than her brother, Ofelia was striking. Her strong, slim body was filled out enough to attract attention wherever she went. Under dark hair her large, violet-gray eyes were set off by light olive-colored skin. They had the same piercing quality as her mind. Never hesitant to speak out, the courage of her convictions matched her gaze.

Pretending Ofelia had not interrupted, Martín continued. "Well, anyway, there's fresh hay in the lofts and in each stall. Then I rode down to Punta del Agua to have Justino Abeyta re-shoe Pizarra. Pretty exciting day, huh? Where's Father?"

As if on cue, a thud came from the Wolfs' bedroom. As he left it, Aaron ricocheted off the door jamb. The three in the *sala* exchanged glances when he walked through the doorway into the *sala* balancing a full glass of tequila and attempting to maintain his dignity.

To try and break the tension, Martín said, "Father, on my way down to Abeyta's in Punta del Agua, I checked the water level in Ojo Gigante for you."

To everyone in the valley water was the major and continuing concern.

"Speaking of checking, how about you checking in at home earlier? This house isn't being run for your convenience." In a softer tone he added, "So how is the flow at old O-jo?" smiling smugly at his rhyming wit.

"Supper will be ready shortly," interrupted Daisy.

Ojo Gigante, a spring on the west side of town at the foot of the Manzanos, was the only source of the village's water supply. Collecting in a large natural stone basin, underground water from the mountains behind fed it. Spillage from the basin flowed into a dammed pond slightly above the level of the town. Though not always a year-round spring,

Ojo Gigante was fairly dependable for village use and watering close-in fields.

Before answering his father's question about the flow from the spring, Martín took a quick look at Aaron's drink and said, "Brimming, as usual," knowing the sarcasm was lost on his father.

"Sounds like you wasted most of your day," he said thickly.

Aaron rarely missed a chance to belittle his son. Martín stared without expression at his father who stared back.

Inches taller than Aaron's six feet and without the bulk he had accumulated, his son's height and Roman nose reminded him of his own hated, dimly remembered father.

Ofelia stepped between her brother and Aaron, placing her hand gently on his arm. "Father, you've had a long day. Why don't you sit down and make that the last drink?"

He shrugged off her hand without answering.

"That's rude!"

Ofelia's eyes glittered with anger. Daisy grimaced. Martín glanced up at the ceiling. The three stood together, awkwardly. Ignoring them, Aaron looked around the *sala* as if seeing it for the first time. He walked over to one of the *bancos* built against the walls and sat down abruptly, not spilling a drop, his collapse cushioned by the *colchon,* a folding mattress on the *banco* for sitting comfort or overnight guest. Aaron rested his head against books in one of the *nichos* built into the thick adobe wall above each *banco.* Jammed with a collection of books second to none south of Santa Fe, the library had ignited his children's passion for reading. Several comfortless chairs and a wood chest for blankets completed the *sala's* furnishings. By valley standards the sparse room was elegant.

Suddenly straightening up, Aaron mumbled to no one in particular, "What's for supper?"

Daisy ignored him and turned to her son.

"Martín, it's cooling off. We need a small fire in here."

He dug kindling and several piñon logs out of the

woodbox and quickly laid and lighted a fire in the beehive-shaped fireplace. Its wrap-around mantel held carved wood *santos*. Above them were *retablos,* religious paintings on wood, hung randomly between kerosene-burning wall sconces.

To hide her nervousness, Daisy called out unnecessary instructions to her kitchen-wise daughter. "Ofelia, those *frijoles* should be hot by now. Put some *tortillas* on the *comal* to warm. That good *carne adovada* you fixed last night is also hot. Should be even better tonight."

Martín smiled with anticipation.

Ofelia's head appeared through the kitchen doorway. "Really, Mother! I know what's for supper." With a sideways look at her father, she added acidly, "It's ready for those who can make it to the table," and began bringing out the food.

The family moved to the dining area at the end of the *sala* and sat down at a simple wood table surrounded by four stiff-backed chairs. Set with bone-handled utensils, earthenware plates and mugs, the table rested on a brown *gerga* rug of coarse wool. Appetites won out over family tension, and for minutes there were only the sounds of eating. With a *tortilla* Martín scooped up the last of his *carne adovada,* and looked carefully to see what his father's mood might be. Supper had sobered him somewhat, and nothing controversial had been said since before supper.

Leaning forward and gesturing at Aaron with the remains of his *tortilla,* he began, "I think cattle, not sheep, are the future here in the valley. To be a cattleman! That's something I'd really like."

"What's wrong with sheep? The family's been doing pretty well on them since before you were born."

"In town I heard that some people from back east have started a cattle operation out at Antelope Springs. Seems they've brought in something like five thousand head. Isn't that a lot more than those springs can water? But they must know what they're doing or they wouldn't have invested all that money."

Aaron's head snapped up sharply, as he looked suspiciously at his son. "How'd you know about that?"

Taken aback, Martín answered, "I just told you, in town."

"Really, Father. Even I know that," said Ofelia. "They've been out there for weeks. Why not talk about cattle? Martín could be right, you know. At least think about it, Father."

Hoping to drive home the point he had been repeating for months, Martín added, "The price of beef keeps going up, which is more than I can say for mutton and wool."

Looking warily at his son, in a thick voice Aaron said, "Who says I'm not interested in cattle? I've got plans for adding more land. Then we'll talk about adding cattle."

Aaron had fifty head now, mainly for beef.

All heads turned in disbelief at Aaron's out-of-the-blue statement. Where would he get more land? How could he afford it, not to mention the cost of buying more cattle?

The sound of hooves in their lane halted conversation. At a knock on the *sala* door Martín started to get up, but Aaron rose quickly, motioning him back into his chair. He opened the front door just wide enough to slip out and closed it hesitantly behind him. He stepped out under the *portal*. Martín got up again and left the room. Outside, Jack Baird, arms crossed over his chest, leaned against a post supporting the *portal*. Behind him, holding their horses, stood Rafe Corcoran.

"What in God's name are you doing here at this time at night? Are you crazy?"

"Jes' wanted to see where you lived, Aa-ron," drawled Baird insultingly.

He stared at the house covetously, admiring its size and the rare glass glazing in the front windows. With a low whistle he stooped to look through the window.

"Lookee here, Rafe!"

Rafe threw the reins over the hitchrail and stepped up in time to help Baird watch the shapely Ofelia take dishes out to the kitchen.

"That your dotter, Aa-ron? She's a looker!"

Leave," said Aaron, angrier by the minute.

"Whitney needs you, old man, Some rancher named McAfee's raising hell about being moved out. Whitney said to get you to help smooth things over."

"Tell Whitney I'll be at McAfee's spread tomorrow afternoon by three. Now get out of here!"

Distracted, trying to hid his confusion, Aaron returned to the table. Martín walked back into the room.

Daisy had her back to the window, not seeing the scene on the porch. She looked at her husband. "Who on earth was that at this time of night?"

He sat down heavily and stared at his plate. Always a poor liar, he said lamely, "Just our sheepherders asking for instructions before taking the flocks out to pasture tomorrow."

Martín said nothing. When he had risen in the morning, the flocks and herders were already on their way. Besides, the hoofbeats in the lane didn't sound at all like those made by the shoeless burros the herders rode. When the door was briefly open, he heard the ring of a spur rowel. Daisy and Ofelia seemed equally skeptical.

Who were they? Could they have something to do with whatever's bothering Father? Why would he lie about them? He didn't like it, but it was his father's business.

CHAPTER 3

EARLY NEXT MORNING, the air already hot, muggy, without a hint of coolness, Martín rose, did his chores at a snail's pace, then fixed breakfast. After oats for Pizarra, he leisurely saddled him, waved goodbye to early-rising Daisy, and rode slowly down into Manzano to chat with his friend Charles Kusz. Kusz was the know-it-all publisher of the valley's only newspaper, controversially named GRINGO & GREASER.

Why Kusz chose to settle in the town of Manzano neither Martín nor anyone else knew. One look at the village's main street was enough to see that the town would never become the hotbed of anything except an occasional brawl, knife fight or murder. Eighty years earlier Manzano had been a valley hamlet defending itself against Navajo and Comanche raids. In fact, the remnants of its *torreon,* a lookout tower of stone and adobe, still rose above all that was left of the town's central plaza and the inevitable, unused communal well.

What little recorded history exists about Manzano suggests that of the more aggressive Indian tribes it was only the Apache who saw long-term benefits in trading rather than raiding, and had been semi-friendly to the Manzaneños. Periodically, Apaches half-heartedly helped beef up Manzano defenses during raids by other aggressive tribes. Fortunately, local *pueblo* Indians, ardently wooed by the church-building Franciscans, got off their knees often and long enough to teach the villagers dry farming and other skills enabling the town to survive.

Unremarkable was the only way to characterize Manzano. "Downtown" consisted of two general stores and opposite them a pair of cantinas that served as social centers and headquarters for the town's two rival political parties. A hundred feet further on was Charles Kusz's combination home and office, and where GRINGO & GREASER was published. Beyond his office an unclaimed orchard managed yearly to produce small, tasteless apples, *manzanas,* from which the village got its name.

Martín watched Kusz, chewing a last bite of breakfast, napkin still tucked into the neck of a collarless shirt, step out his front door to check the weather. His head missed the hand-adzed lintel by a scant inch as he ducked back inside. Moments later he reappeared adjusting garters on his sleeves, and paper cuffs to minimize the inevitable inkstains hazarded by newspaper editors. With dark hair parted in the middle, slimly built, of medium height, Kusz radiated nervous energy. Though Martín doubted they were needed, Kusz insisted on wearing wire-rimmed glasses, hoping they would give him the scholarly look he wanted to effect.

Charles Kusz was easily Manzano's most baffling resident. The town had divided opinions as to whether he was crazy or just strange. GRINGO & GREASER was the most outrageous name he could have chosen for his newspaper in an area where, at best, relations between Mexicans and Anglo-Americans were strained. Yet its editorial and news content was surprisingly even-handed. The semi-monthly, bilingual paper had an odd size, 8-1/2 x 14", dictated by the small, obsolete, surplus U.S. Army press on which it was printed. The paper was set entirely in italics, the only complete type font Kusz had been able to purchase at a bargain price.

Sitting quietly on Pizarra, Martín was not hard to spot.

Kusz smiled and waved. "I hope you've got a good reason for being down here this hot morning."

"*Buenas Dias,* Charles. The best — to visit you. I see you're putting on work clothes. Have you got a few minutes? I need your advice."

Kusz stood up a little straighter at the compliment. "Always got time for you. Come on into the office. Too damn hot out here."

Martín ducked under the lintel and, following Kusz, threaded his way through the chaos of a large room combining dining area, kitchen, several type trays and the printing press. Slipping onto a high stool in front of a tilted type tray, Kusz pivoted around to face his friend. Kusz's willingness to talk about anything, and he had strong opinions about everything, attracted Martín the most. There was always plenty of chatter and gossip at home, but seldom solid, thought-provoking conversation. When Charles and Martín first met, they spent hours talking, legs dangling over the edge of the natural stone basin of Ojo Gigante. Mainly the talk was about Kusz.

Born into a liberal New York State family in 1849, at twenty-six, college behind him, Kusz went west to Georgetown, Colorado, where, reputedly, fortunes in gold were just waiting to be made. He became a notary public, tried his hand at real estate and the hotel business, then finally managed to maneuver himself onto the outer fringe of the gold and silver mining boom. At fabled Fryer's Hill in Leadville, Colorado, he struck it rich. Shortly afterward, his wife of four years and most of his small fortune fled together.

Kusz felt better about his loss when he found how the miners who made him modestly wealthy were being shamelessly exploited by others who supplied the labor. In a community atmosphere of total racial prejudice, poverty-stricken Mexicans and Chinese worked for pennies an hour. Exploitation and bigotry cut deeply across Kusz's liberal grain. He tried to do something about it — writing — but local Colorado newspapers refused to publish him. So, with some writing talent and what remained of his money, he drifted south into New Mexico and put both to work as one of the first journalists in the Estancia Valley.

There he found the cause he needed and grist for his liberal mill; Mexicans and Americans continuously at each other's throats over a host of issues. Charles Kusz was the first to even try reporting favorably on the Mexican lifestyle. And printing his paper in both English and Spanish immediately guaranteed him a larger audience. The pattern of what was to come showed up in one of the earliest issues of GRINGO & GREASER.

He wrote, "Mexican betrothals are of a primitive fashion —. Young folks have little to say in their selection of life partners —. But for all that, Mexican couples seem to be as well matched as any others."

A workaholic, Kusz spread himself too thin, a trait Martín commented on to no avail. Besides publishing GRINGO & GREASER, he again became a notary public, ran a small cattle ranch, an assay office for the local mining industry, a store, was Manzano's postmaster and became commissioner of immigration for Valencia County. Kusz and young Martín got acquainted when, then working in a hard rock mine, he brought a quartz sample into Kusz's office to be assayed for gold content. Kusz instantly liked the well-read young man, and their friendship took off.

He picked up several proof sheets off the type tray, squinted at Martín, and handed him the top one. "Before you start asking me your important philosophic questions, give me your opinion on a couple of things I've just written. I hope you think this first one is as funny as I do."

Martín studied the sheet. It read, "An Eastern drug paper goes into ecstasy over a sponge weighing 11 pounds. Pshaw! Come west, young man, and see the sights! While in Santa Fe last week, we saw more than fifty sponges at the leading hotels and boarding houses, any one of them weighing from 150 to 200 pounds."

He chuckled. "That is funny."

Kusz handed him another sheet. "This is also supposed to be funny, but I don't think it'll win me any friends here in town."

Martín quickly read the proof. "Manzano is one of the oldest towns in the Territory, hence everybody has confidence in its stability. Its style of architecture is mud gothic. The alleys and bullyvards (sic) are lit by Jersey Lightning (liquor) and tanglefoot gas. Manzano is the center of paper railways, grapevine telegraphs and old women telephones. The sanitary condition of the town is immense, especially in the healthy season. It is famous for its weather, hardly ever being without a spell. Its trade extends in every direction except upwards and outwards."

With a smile he handed the sheet back to his friend. "Since it's already typeset, I guess you're going to run it. If I didn't live around here, that piece would be pretty funny, too."

Kusz twisted a bit on his stool, leaned back against a type tray and dropped his hands in his lap.

"Thanks for the encouragement. Yes, I'm going to run both of them. Now, it's your turn."

"Charles, you know that what I really want to do is to be in the cattle ranching business. Specially where I can be part of the group that runs it, not just a hired hand. You're a fountain of knowledge. Who do you know who's doing something in the cattle ranching, anywhere, that I might talk to?"

"I thought you'd been in the cattle business and didn't like it."

"Come on, Charles. I don't mean that *rico* gringo rancher in the north valley. That was a wasted year."

" Just teasing. First, how about some coffee? It's not all that great, but it'll keep you awake while I talk."

Kusz poured two cups of the strong hot brew that looked and tasted like printer's ink.

He leaned back again, took a sip, grimaced, and said, "They 're a lot of small cattle outfits in the valley that don't need any help. Two, I believe, will become fairly significant. One is large for this valley, the other just starting up, but I'm sure will grow. Both have a problem. In fact, the same problem — land. Each are claiming the same piece of ground."

"That's got to be the Whitney and Otero operations."

"Right. Mostly you hear about the Whitneys, a couple of *rico* brothers from back in New England."

"Didn't they just push a lot of cattle into Antelope Springs?"

"Right again. And that's another of their problems. They're naive about cattle and think all you have to have is money. At some point they'll learn cows can't drink or eat it. Now, Otero's different. His plans don't seem to be completely formed yet, but I know he's got ambitions to be a significant cattle rancher. I guess you and your father know him as the honcho of the valley's biggest sheep outfit."

"Yes. Father used to see the older Oteros at stock sales. 'They're crusty but honest,' he'd say."

Kusz continued. "What you probably don't know is that Otero has already added a few hundred cattle to his valley sheep operation out at his ranch at Estancia Springs. Sort of a seed herd, I think.

"Doesn't Otero own that big old *estancia* on the edge of the Rio Grande? South of where I used to go to school in Tome?"

"Yep. Inherited the place from his father. Anyway, both of these outfits will need good men to help them grow, though the Whitneys probably don't know it yet. You might talk to them, though. They just may get smart and the operation takes off. If you're a mind to, go see James Whitney. He's the younger brother, the only one out here, and runs the operation."

"Where do you get all this information, Charles?"

"Just flows in my direction. To be completely candid," continued Kusz, "you ought to know how Whitney's operating. He's throwing small outfits off land they've been on for years, even generations. 'Squatters' he calls them. Some have been squatting so long they probably now have a legal right to be there. Those he can't push out, he buys out."

"If he's that high-handed, why should I talk to Whitney? Don't like the sound of him."

"Honestly, Martín, they're not many places to look for the kind of job you want. If you can stomach Whitney's approach, you've doubled your chances of finding a job."

"Is Whitney doing the strong-arming himself?"

"Hardly. To add muscle to his operation, he's hired seven *Tejano* gunslingers. I think they're human debris left over after the Lincoln County War a few years back. Heard that when they aren't leaning on squatters for Whitney, these lads are using free time to do things in their own interest."

"Like what?"

"Use your imagination. Ever thought about how many loose cattle there are in the valley?"

I hope Charles doesn't talk this candidly to anybody else, thought Martín. Those *Tejanos* might not take too kindly to that.

"So you've told me what you think about Whitney. How about Otero?"

"Besides being smart, he's a gentleman. And he knows a lot more about stock, water, grass and weather in the valley than Whitney ever will. Instead of throwing money at a cattle build-up, he's taking a step at a time. Now *there's* a man who'd be worth riding over to La Constancia and talking to. Something else you ought to know."

"You're going to tell me about a land grant problem between Whitney and Otero. I've heard a little about it.

"You're reading my mind. Am I boring you?"

"Hardly. I don't know any of the details. Besides, I love to hear you talk, especially when you know what you're talking about."

Kusz took the teasing with a smile and said, "What would you do if a former Mexican governor granted you a million acres which you 'proved up' over several years thinking it was yours. Then suddenly, the next Mexican governor gives half of that land to somebody else?"

"I'd be furious and fight like hell to get it back."

"Of course you would," said Charles. "Around 1821 the then-Mexican governor granted a million acres to a man named Baca. In 1845 Manuel Armijo, the unpredictable, unlamented, last Mexican governor of New Mexico, gave half of Baca's million acres to a man named Sandoval. In the 1850s, after the Americans had taken over New Mexico, it turns out that a U.S. commission discovered that Governor Armijo had been trafficking in a lot of other illegal grants besides the Baca."

"Baca and his heirs must have been furious!"

"To say the least! To add to the confusion, Sandoval, to make a quick peso, turned around and sold the grant to his wealthy nephew."

Suddenly he stopped talking. Mouth open, he stared fixedly out the mullioned glass window. Martín turned and saw why. Two well-armed men had ridden so close to it their horses' breaths fogged the glass panes. Threateningly yet unmoving, they stared only at Kusz.

Trying to make light of the situation, Martín said, "Friends of yours?"

"God, I hope not! Never seen those hombres before. Sure don't seem friendly to me."

After a last hard look at Kusz, the riders slowly rode away. He exhaled. Martín was certain he knew more about these men than he wanted to say.

Kusz passed a hand over his eyes and with effort said, "Where was I? Oh, yes. In the '70s and in good faith, the two Otero brothers — that's the father and uncle of young Otero — bought the original million acres granted to Baca."

"But you said half that land had already been given to somebody else by the last Mexican governor."

"Right. The Oteros knew that, but were certain that Governor Armijo's grant was illegal. In fact, to sew up their claim, one of the brothers went all the way to Mexico City to get the original deed from the Baca heirs."

Kusz rubbed his face and looked at Martín. "Who do you think those hard cases were?"

He couldn't help.

Kusz blinked, then continued. "Well, anyway, Sandoval's nephew recently sold the disputed half-million acres to the Whitney boys. Then both Otero brothers died. So young Manuel Otero is squared off against the Whitneys over the half-million acres. By the way, Manuel Otero inherited only a third of the original grant. His two brothers-in-law got the other two-thirds. Are you following all this?"

"Sort of."

"So now the Whitneys have five thousand head of cattle on this disputed land trying to water them at Antelope Springs where there's not enough for half that. But the land they bought includes Otero's Estancia Springs ranch where there's plenty of water. Otero and the Whitneys are holding their breaths waiting for the Santa Fe court to decide who owns what. Something's bound to happen soon. Cattle can't go for long without water."

"Sticky situation!"

"That's putting it mildly. Both sides say the other's claim wasn't properly recorded. People around here were so casual about recording deeds that both parties could be right."

"So who's going to win?"

"If I knew that, I wouldn't be in the newspaper business. All I know is that I like Manuel Otero and the way he does things."

CHAPTER 4

DETERMINED TO GET INTO THE CATTLE BUSINESS, to Martín a forty-five-mile ride to La Constancia, Otero's spread on the Rio Grande, didn't seem all that much of an effort. There and back would take about four days, he guessed. If he got lucky and was asked to stay over, maybe seven. How could he better spend a week? Only his mother knew where he was going and for how long he'd be gone. Not telling his father was gutless, but the less they had to do with each other the better. Daisy agreed that more acrimony and arguments would help neither.

At two in the morning of the day after his talk with Kusz, Martín stepped from his bedroom onto the patio to check the weather. The before-dawn July day was misted over and cool. An indistinct three-quarter moon seemed moored just above the haze. Once the sun burned through, he knew it would be scorching, hardly the best weather for a long ride.

Nothing but his best clothes, the only other ones he had, would do for meeting Otero. Opening the warped door of his hand-me-down *trastero,* Martín groped inside by the light of a candle. He brought out *calzones,* a black pantaloon with silver conchos down each leg. From off a hook he lifted *botas,* smart-looking leggings worn below the knee to prevent chafing on a long ride. Fortunately, his only linen shirt was clean. To wear over it, he pulled out a black vest with intricately carved bone buttons. Rolling the clothes with care, he tied them compactly in an oilcloth cover. Slipping on everyday heavy cotton pants, he then shrugged into a shirt of the same material, and used a cloth bag to hold a clean but wrinkled cotton shirt, fresh underwear and shaving gear. After a moment's thought, he lifted down from the wall a carefully maintained Winchester '73, the sole occupant of an antelope-hoof rifle rack, and from under the bed fished out a full box of shells. A last glance told him he had forgotten nothing. Palming out the candle, he stocking-footed noiselessly down the hall to the kitchen.

Dry piñon roots added to still-glowing coals in the stove enabled him to blow alive a small fire with just enough warmth to heat leftover coffee, *tortillas, frijoles* and *carne adovada* excavated from the bottom of the clay *tinaje*. In a canvas sack went the last of the *tortillas* and some parched corn. After filling his canteen at the kitchen pump, he stepped out onto the puncheon floor under the *portal*, quietly closed the kitchen door and slipped into the high-topped boots he was carrying.

Cautiously, he felt his way to the stable in the pitch dark. With sure hands he found and lighted the lantern, and squatted to scratch Felita's ears until she was content and quiet. Pizarra, watered, noisily munched oats from a leather nose bag while Martín rubbed him down with burlap sacking. For a moment they stood, heads together, enjoying each other's company.

He whispered, "This'll be a long ride, old friend, but maybe worth it for both of us."

Over the Navajo saddle blanket he cinched his comfortable Mexican saddle. On its right side, between stirrup strap and fender, he lashed a rifle scabbard. Into it went the Winchester, butt forward, breech down. Behind the cantle he tied a pair of saddle bags, slipped rifle shells and the canvas sack of food into one, clothes into the other. Over both went a wool poncho. From the large flat horn he hung his canteen and extra oats in a nose bag. Pizarra's bridle in place, throat-latch buckled, Martín blew out the lantern and led the horse outside.

As he mounted, Pizarra threw his head, snorted approval of the cool morning, then minced sideways into the dark to begin the long trip to the Rio Grande. The road through Manzano and the five miles to Punta del Agua they covered at a fast walk.

Exhilarated by the prospects ahead, Martín called out loud to the coming day, "You've been a long time getting here!" though he knew in his heart he was far from being "here" yet. From the moment he could first straddle a horse, his ambition had been to be a cattle rancher. Not like the New Mexico Territory's legendary Lucien Maxwell lording over tens of thousands of acres and countless head of stock. All he wanted was just some land with grass, not necessarily the best, a seed herd of cattle and a few horses. Each seemed basic and wholesome and tapped a vein of longing deep inside of him. Land and stock required money, lots of it. He had none. But ambition in the young, like love, is often blind to realities. In some yet-to-be-revealed way he was certain these obstacles would be overcome.

At Punta del Agua Martín pulled up Pizarra and made a decision that almost proved fatal. The easy way to the Rio Grande was around the southern end of the Manzanos, then west through Abo Pass. If he took a chance on the only shortcut, more than four hours of riding would be saved.

The shortcut, little known except to him and a few other hunters, was a trail through the heart of the southern Manzanos. For centuries Indians, migrating on foot from the Rio Grande east into the Estancia Valley, had worn smooth a narrow, rocky path up Cañon Barranco. From Punta del Agua a short ride west over a few rolling hills brought them to the precipitous trail down into the canyon. In daylight the Cañon Barranco trail was tricky and difficult. By moonlight, its hazards would be multiplied. To rationalize the choice of the shortcut, he decided that just as going to see Otero was taking a chance, so was this.

And he felt lucky.

Mostly led by Martín, surefooted Pizarra felt his way down the steepest part of the descent. The moon, perversely ducking in and out of thickening clouds mustering above them, was scant help. At the foot of the steep descent they turned due west into the mouth of Cañon Espinosa. Swallowing hard, he looked back with relief and almost disbelief at the trail they had just descended. Early morning light began to take over from dawn. The strain of the descent had been exhausting. He knew Pizarra was as tired as he was.

They walked to Ojo Abo, a year-round spring a few miles further down the arroyo. There he watered and grazed Pizarra. The twisting corridors of Cañon de Abo lay ahead, but would be easy compared to what they had covered in virtual darkness. He estimated about twenty-five more miles would bring him to La Constancia.

As they entered the canyon, he watched uneasily as the sky changing rapidly from a sallow yellow to an ominous gray. The wind picked up. From virtually none, it began to flowing with intimidating force. Funneled by canyon walls, gusts rocketed eastward directly into their faces, pummeling them with debris lifted from the canyon floor. Gashes of lightning probed the Manzanos. The shearing sound of thunder ricocheted off steep cliffs and rolled toward them, amplified as it approached. Dense clouds, lightning and thunder combined to summon a driving monsoon rain, more typical of late summer than July.

Too late he realized the shortcut was a terrible choice. Doubling back now would be virtually impossible. He envisioned a flash flood in the narrow confines of the canyon. Riders he knew of had been swept away. In less than two miles the canyon widened, he remembered. Pizarra could outrun any flood! That was not being honest with himself. Only he had committed them to the canyon. As their lack of options became starkly apparent, lightning struck so close they were engulfed by the pungent smell of ozone. Panicked by the flash, acrid odor and almost instantaneous shatter of thunder, Pizarra reared. Deep in his saddle Martín fought for control, narrowly avoiding their capsizing backwards.

Rowelling Pizarra for the first time on the ride, he had no trouble coaxing the terrified horse into a cautious lope down the canyon's boulder-strewn floor. Rain fell, first in enormous drops, then in blinding torrents. Its impact on them increased with their speed. Curtains of rain propelled by the wind turned cold. While on the run Martín managed to untie the wool *serape* lashed behind his cantle. As he slipped the cape over his head, the wind bellied it out behind him, badly spooking the horse. Pizarra almost lost his footing in sand and dirt rapidly turning into a greasy, sucking mud. Their path down the canyon took them directly into the gullet of the storm.

The shallow creek they followed, normally trickling at a leisurely pace west through the canyon, deepened. At first imperceptibly, while the rain slaked the parched canyon floor, then more quickly. As the stream rose, so did his concern for their safety. The steep walls of the two-hundred-foot-wide canyon denied them any escape. Martin tried to keep Pizarra on a sandy ledge paralleling the rising stream, but the fragile shelf dissolved under his hooves. Then came the first turbulence of water warning of the flood cresting behind it. Just audible above the battering of the rain and the water's rush began a drumming sound, not unlike buffalo running over rocky ground. It became a thumping, grinding, crackling of boulders scoured from the canyon floor, rolled like pebbles in the overpowering flood of water.

As Martín knew it would, Cañon de Abo began to widen. But so did the rapidly rising stream. Water spreading and deepening forced them to hug the canyon wall. As a last resort, he reined Pizarra up onto a rock shelf above the roiling stream, stopped and held his breath. This was their only chance for safety. Crossing himself, he prayed, *"Dios, nos salve."* Terrified, the horse cast a wild eye down at the flooding creek. A foot below where they pressed against the canyon wall its crest swept by. Branches and roots of full-grown trees, ripped whole from the soil, clutched at the gray's legs as they passed in the grip of the water's remorseless energy.

Then the crest was downstream of them. The water level began to drop. Like a suddenly idled pump, the monsoon downpour slowed and, as quickly as it began, stopped. Even through the thick leather of the saddle fenders, Martín could feel Pizarra's heart pumping hard, almost in rhythm with his own. Both were exhausted by the effort and terror, both unsteady on their legs. Martín dismounted and ran his hand under the horse's jaw, then down its nose, trying to calm Pizarra as well as himself. Wringing out the soaking *serape,* he re-lashed it behind his cantle. It was impossible to re-shape his wilted straw *sombrero,* remarkably still on his head. The creek quickly shrank to its original size.

When it appeared safe, a newly cautious Martín led Pizarra half-walking, half-sliding their way down and out of the canyon's steep mouth.

Looking at the sun suddenly released by the passing storm, he figured it close to eleven o'clock. On the move for almost eight hours and they were still little more than halfway to La Constancia. So much for the shortcut! At a minimum, twenty burning miles and the hottest part of the day lay ahead of them. He was tempted to push on with the still nervous and flighty Pizarra. Despite the horse's almost legendary endurance, it would be cruel to continue. Otero didn't know Martín or have any idea he was coming. So what was the hurry?

CHAPTER 5

JUST BEYOND THE MOUTH of the canyon they came to a well-grassed, sloping meadow bisected by the now gentled stream. A high bluff partly shaded the area from cruel afternoon sun. He led the still agitated horse into the shady portion and picketed him on a long rope to give plenty of room for grazing. In minutes Martín gathered and spread out to dry an armful of wood, part of the debris scattered by the flooding creek. Padded by his heavy *serape,* he leaned against a rock to watch a hawk ride a thermal up the bluff's almost vertical face.

Sleepily, he tried to calculate his chances of success with Otero. At the least they'd be no worse than the first ranching job he took. What a sickening, memorable year. He should have known it would be when the American-Anglo, whose spread was in the north valley near Buffalo Springs, insisted on being called *"patron."* Twenty-one, Martín was fed up with sheep and his father. His new boss lived down to Martín's minimum expectations. On discovering he was *coyote,* a half-Mexican, half-Anglo, the *patron* took delight in badgering him.

"Which half of you is Anglo? You look all-greaser to me."

Then he would howl like a coyote, laughing at his riotous sense of humor. Out of the question was Martín's working with cattle. But if the job was menial or filthy enough, it was his. Sustained only by pride, clenched fists and silence, he endured barely a year.

Roused from his daydream, he moved Pizarra's picket pin to a fresh area in the meadow, took a long drink in the stream and returned to his comfortable seat against the bluff. A cascade of rocks nearby convinced him to move away from its face.

Why had he gone back to work for his father? At the time he remembered thinking that compared to the cattle ranch, five thousand acres of good grass grazing three thousand sheep looked pretty attractive. A bad choice as it turned out. Just another year of being a well-paid hand with boarding privileges. The daily "I told you so's" from Aaron clinched it. He quit his father's employ again.

Harvesting timber-rich ravines in the Manzano mountains was the valley's only industry with any promise. His job started off well, though operations were primitive and heavily dependent on muscle power. Intrigued by the possibilities of a permanent position, he signed on for work and accommodations as rough as the all-Mexican crew. The *gringo* boss expected every man to instantly become a lumberjack-of-all-trades: felling trees, trimming limbs, bucking logs to length, then, behind skittish mule teams, skidding logs down impossibly steep slopes to a landing far below.

For recreation there were only three choices: story telling, drinking or fighting. Well-read Martín was a natural spinner of yarns. What liquor made its way into camp was cheap, short on euphoria, long on headaches. Drinking sooner or later meant fighting, generally with a knife.

Martín was surprised to discover he had talent as a knife fighter. *Machismo*, that inbred Mexican requirement to prove one's manhood, meant everyone, at least once, had to challenge and be overmatched by the newly discovered talent of agile, long-armed Wolf. Most fights he was goaded into. All were for trivial reasons or imagined insults. His opponent was usually drunk, he sober. Without exception he won, though stopping when the slightest scratch was inflicted. *Machismo* was satisfied with just a show of blood.

At the urging of his crew-mates, he bought a knife, a second-hand Green River "Arkansas Toothpick," stiletto-shaped, with a twelve-inch blade, both edges honed to razor sharpness. A sharp knife makes a cleaner wound, he found. As did others in the crew, he wore it, then and now, in a scabbard on the back of his belt.

To Martín some tree harvesting practices used time-wasting methods that could be easily remedied. Here, he thought, was a great opportunity to impress the *patron*. In retrospect, how could he have been so naive to think the Anglo-American boss of the timber camp would listen to his suggestions?

One day, *sombrero* in hand, he walked into the owner's flimsy shack.

"*Patron,* if you'll pardon my saying," he began modestly, "we could get logs to the landing quicker and cheaper than we do now. And we wouldn't keep killing mule teams like we did again yesterday."

"I suppose you have something brilliant in mind," said the owner sarcastically.

Taken aback, Martín pressed on quietly.

"What if we string a temporary cable down to the landing from where we're cutting. With a simple cradle on it, we could run the logs down and pull the cradle back up with mule power. It'd be easy to restring the rig when we move to a new cutting area."

Why wouldn't he welcome a simple, cost-saving solution like that, he thought. The boss gave him a hard look. Martín was making sense, but the *patron* was embarrassed to have been out-thought by a Mexican.

"I been in this business ten years. Don't need no greaser to tell me how the work should be done. Go back to work."

His budding enthusiasm for lumbering rudely extinguished, Martín turned to hard rock mining. Except that they didn't have as much fun, the all-Mexican crew at the mine was interchangeable with the one he had just left. They were under another unbending Anglo-American boss/owner, and work conditions were even worse. Handling dynamite that sweated its nitroglycerine on a hot day seemed a poor way to fulfill his ambition for a career. There was unexpected compensation. Sent to Manzano to have an ore sample assayed, he met Charles Kusz. Their friendship developed quickly and made his brief career in mining seem at least worth something.

An empty stomach and the setting sun cut short his daydreaming and prompted him to make a small fire for coffee and to heat up his meager store of rations. Wrapped in the utilitarian wool poncho, he settled down for a peaceful night. So peaceful that next morning, with the sun well over the Manzanos, restless Pizarra pulled his picket and wandered over to thrust a moist muzzle into Martín's motionless form. Reaction was immediate. He sat bolt upright, embarrassed to have been caught oversleeping, even by his horse. He washed his face and drank deeply from the stream, then fingered dampened hair back into place. Pizarra contentedly munched oats from a nosebag. With a cold *tortilla* in his mouth, he quickly saddled and bridled the horse and swung lightly into the saddle. The sun told him it was about eight in the morning.

Ahead lay a virtually featureless plain unrolling more than twenty miles to the Rio Grande. Nothing broke the western horizon save the faint outline of the San Mateo mountains some seventy miles distant. Occasional mounds of rocks partially hidden in sandy caliche relieved the flat, high desert landscape. Only scattered clumps of chamisa, cholla, yucca and prickly pear cactus prospered in the inhospitable soil. Early morning did little to check the searing July heat. In an hour it would be worse. The almost-barren plain baking at oven temperatures would torment both horse and rider all the way across the Belen and Colorado grants. If he kept the sun over his left shoulder, with luck Martín might just come close to La Constancia. A good sense of direction helped him do just that. From the bluffs edging the burning plain he looked beyond Otero's *estancia* to the cool ribbon of the Rio Grande.

La Constancia's extensive acreage sloped gently west to the river's edge. When at school in Tome, he had barely noticed the *estancia*, but now recognized the north-south dirt road he often took along its eastern edge. The large adobe to the north had to be the Otero *hacienda*. South of it lay outbuildings and shops, a large barn, corral and cattle pens. Further south an orchard bordered fields of corn, wheat and cotton. West of these was the *pueblito,* a tiny village of clustered adobes enclosing a minute plaza and well, alive with women, children, men probably too old or sick to work, dogs, chickens and pigs. On the other side of a fence running from the *hacienda* to the *pueblito*, grazing lands dipped gently toward a *bosque,* a thin screen of trees edging the Rio Grande. Pasturage did not seem to be very lush, but the horses and cattle he could see were sleek and healthy. Sheep at the far end of the pasture were being watched by dogs and small boys trying hard to act like adult herders.

Martín dismounted and squatted for a longer look at the *hacienda*. Heavy-walled, utilitarian, the blocky structure seemed almost dug into the earth from which its bricks were made. More a fort than home, it lay several hundred yards west of a poorly maintained split-rail fence paralleling the dirt road. On the rear portion of the *hacienda* a second story had been built, probably for the bedrooms to catch any breeze off the river.

From local history taught at Father Ralliere's school, Martín remembered that less than three decades earlier the Navajo were using the Rio Grande Valley as a turnpike, raiding ranches for slaves and livestock. No wonder the *hacienda* looked like a fort! Outside its heavy walls was yet another, a high adobe enclosure yards away from the house that had apparently originally completely surrounded it. The wall on the river side of the *hacienda* had been pulled down.

Enough looking! He had come to ask for a job. What kind of man would he find Otero to be? How could one person own all this and part of the Baca Grant and be untouched by wealth and power?

With the last of his canteen water he rinsed his face, then pulled from the saddlebag the roll of clean "job hunting" clothes and slipped into them almost self-consciously. Remounting Pizarra, he rode carefully down the steep bluff to the front gate of the *hacienda*. Any questions he had about Otero or job possibilities would soon be answered.

CHAPTER 6

ONLY A HANDFUL of *estancias* owned by Mexicans were left in New Mexico Territory. All were holdovers from the Spanish period, generally anachronistic in equipment and farming methods. Unlike most, La Constancia was run efficiently enough to avoid bankruptcy or a buy-out by Anglo-Americans for debt. Developed on land granted to Manuel Otero's great-grandfather by the king of Spain in the late eighteenth century, over the years it had been gradually improved with the single objective of making the *estancia* self-sufficient.

Its fourth and current *patron* was Manuel B. Otero. Thirty-nine, born into wealth, red-headed, blue-eyed, he could, if he wished, boast of direct lineage from the Spanish. When his father and uncle died two years previously, he inherited all of La Constancia and a third of the Baca Grant in the Estancia Valley. His education, college in St. Louis, Missouri, and graduate work at the University of Heidelberg in Germany, was of no practical use to him as a farmer and rancher. But he learned those trades quickly and took his responsibilities seriously.

In just months Otero realized how much his success depended on all the men, women, even children living on the *estancia*. He felt personally responsible for them, sending a gift for each wedding and birth, attending every funeral. Otero's concern for his workers' health was an anomaly among the few remaining Mexican *patrons*. Frequently, they expressed their opinion about his "coddling" workers. To do less made poor humanitarian and business sense to him. For whatever combination of reasons, La Constancia prospered.

In addition to interest in the workers, and unlike his father and uncle, his courteous manner made him genuinely liked by them and their families. Not born into nobility, he was nevertheless thought of as *hidalgo,* a man of noble birth. Temper was his major flaw. Saved for the incompetent, employee or peer, most victims knew they deserved his outbursts.

* * * * *

Martín was surprised that his approach to the *hacienda* had been noticed. Almost before he could pull his clothes out of the saddlebags and rifle out of its boot, a young *mozo* materialized at the front gate and led away the reluctant Pizarra. Moments later a courteous Mexican, apparently the mayordomo, emerged.

"*Quien es?"* he asked. Martín's height, bearing and unblinking blue eyes convinced the mayordomo this was no ordinary visitor.

"I'm Martín Wolf of Manzano to see don Manuel Otero when it meets his convenience."

With a slight bow, the man replied, "I'm Tranquilo Villareal, the mayordomo. Please follow me."

He led the way into the *hacienda* through the *zaguan* out of which he had come. Wide enough for horse-drawn wagons to pass to protection inside, the *zaguan* was a covered corridor running from the *hacienda's* front wall to the safety of its central patio. With Indian raids only a memory, its usefulness had ceased. A huge pair of solid mesquite gates still sealed its front. Martín stepped over a worn sill and ducked through the small door cut into one of the gates. He glanced back at the heavy forged strap hinges and sturdy mesquite bars securing them. Ahead, the stone-floored corridor led into a paved patio. Centered in it was a *cantera* stone fountain bubbling into a large basin. At the patio's far end he glimpsed a section of tiled *portal* roof.

Halfway down the passageway Villareal gestured Martín through a door on the left matching one on the right. He stepped into what appeared to be Manuel Otero's office. The mayordomo left him there and disappeared to inform don Manuel of his visitor. Martín put his bag of clothing on the floor and leaned the rifle against a wall.

Behind a Victorian desk of dark mahogany a locked gun cabinet held rifles and shotguns. Flanking it was a display of antique arms: wheel lock and flintlock muskets, pistols, caplock rifles and sidearms, all hung from decorative hand-forged nails driven into the adobe wall. Opposite the desk was a comfortable-looking, frequently used horsehair-covered couch. Brass kerosene sconces sporting etched glass chimneys were intricately fastened onto the walls.

One office window looked east out of the front of the building onto the high adobe wall surrounding the *hacienda*. Another faced south, again at an adobe wall, but this one relieved by the greenery of a narrow vineyard between the outer wall and the *hacienda*. To the west a window opened onto the patio. From the depth of the window openings, *hacienda* walls appeared to be nearly three feet thick.

Otero appeared quickly, bowed, apologized for his infinitesimal delay, and without hesitation held out his hand.

"Aaron Wolf must be your father. I've met him several times. He has a reputation for breeding outstanding horseflesh."

Martín just smiled, unable to think of an appropriate reply.

Otero continued. "You've had a long ride. Get caught in that storm yesterday?"

"Certainly did, and for a while wondered if I was going to make it here."

"Why don't you have supper with us and spend the night? You didn't ride all this way for a meal, so how else can I help you?"

Martín suspected Otero valued directness. Abandoning his rehearsed speech, he plunged in. "I understand you're adding cattle at your Estancia Springs ranch. Perhaps my experience can be of help to you with the build-up."

Manuel liked the looks of this direct young man, but was surprised by his question.

Suggesting it would be better to talk business after supper, he said, "Perhaps you'd like a bath and rest before you join us at six. Tranquilo will show you the way to your room."

Villareal, waiting outside Otero's office door, was given brief instructions. With Martín following, Tranquilo led the way down the hall to the rear of the *hacienda* and up to its second floor. At the top of the stairs a corridor ran the width of the house. Doors from it led into four adjoining bedrooms. The first was Martín's, airy, comfortable, with a louvered door opening onto a shallow balcony overlooking the Rio Grande. The balcony, which ran the full width of the building, was divided into segments each as wide as the bedroom it served.

A copper hip tub in the corner of Martín's room was quickly filled with hot water brought by Tranquilo, who disappeared with his soiled clothes. After a long soak he toweled off, lay down for a moment's rest and promptly fell asleep. His last waking thought was that Otero at least had not said "no." What seemed only moments later he was wakened by a discreet knock. Wrapped in a towel, Martín opened the door to find a woman with a pleasant smile and his clothes, somewhat damp but freshly washed and ironed.

She curtsied and murmured, *"La cena sera un media hora,"* as she handed over his clothes.

So far nothing had happened the way Martín had expected. Supper was sure to be another surprise, undoubtedly a trial for his country manners. Promptly at six he found Otero standing at the foot of the stairs. Gently he steered Martín by the elbow into the *sala* which, like the adjacent *comedor,* was on the first floor below the bedrooms. There Otero introduced him to his wife doña Margarita and daughter Catalina.

As Martín bowed to touch his lips to the back of doña Margarita's extended hand, he murmured, *"Estoy encantado,"* and did the same with Catalina. Then he raised his head for a closer look. Soft reddish hair framed a strong oval face. Cool green eyes gazed steadily into his. He blushed to find himself still clinging to her hand. To ease the awkwardness, Otero poured sherry for all. With glass extended toward Martín, he said, *"Mi casa es su casa."*

Just then a stocky young man strode briskly into the room. Instantly apparent was that he and Otero didn't like each other. Otero poured another sherry with obvious reluctance. After a stiff bow to the Oteros and a dark look at Martín, the young man kissed Catalina possessively on the cheek as though he did it every day. Apparently not, for she recoiled with a grimace.

"Martín, Teofilo Armijo's father is my brother-in-law Carlos Armijo. Teo is something of a permanent resident here. Learning farming and ranching. Teo, Martín Wolf will be visiting for a few days."

Martín's impression was that even a few days would be too many for Teo. Fortunately, Otero didn't mention the real purpose of his visit. A bit stiff-legged, as if he sensed a potential rival, Teo finally shook Martín's proffered hand.

To get Teo to talk about anything at all was like drawing nails driven in hardwood. After several attempts by Martín to start a conversation, Teo finally broke his silence with a flat statement.

"My father lives in Albuquerque. He's in the wholesale grain business and owns a third of the Baca Grant."

More questioning disclosed the fact that Teo's main interest was money. Also, that his father, Carlos, and Otero's wife, Margarita, had persuaded a reluctant Otero to take Teo on as an unpaid apprentice. Margarita and her brother Carlos hoped the *estancia* would ignite Teo's interests. Apparently, Carlos also hoped that, although they were first cousins, Teo's stay would ignite Catalina's interest in his son. From what Martín could see, La Constancia had lighted no fires under Teo and certainly not in Catalina.

In an odd aside, Teo whispered to Martín, "Considering all the work I do around here, Uncle Manuel should pay me."

To minimize mistakes in his manners, Martín watched and copied the Oteros closely. Either they were being polite by not noticing his, or he made few serious blunders. But even he knew Teo's manners were gross.

When asked what his middle name was, Martín grinned and said "Romulo." No one associated "Romulo" with his last name "Wolf." So he told the story of the she-wolf suckling Romulus and Remus and the founding of Rome.

"I should know," he said pointing. "This is what's called a Roman nose. Maybe I'm part Italian."

The Oteros threw back their heads and laughed. Teo sat in stony silence.

Hard pressed to keep his eyes off Catalina directly opposite him, he guessed she was seventeen or eighteen, though with the self-assurance of a woman years older. Her body was as captivating as her face and manner. It looked strong without the exaggerated curves of most young Mexican women he knew. Full breasts filled out the bodice of a dress which, he learned later, she had embroidered herself. They were accentuated when she leaned against the table to emphasize a point. Yet she seemed unaffected by her beauty. No wonder Teo paid her such close attention!

Little attention was paid to Teo whenever he joined the conversation. Martín quickly understood why. Teo was a bore. Most of what he had to say was about himself. At one point the left side of his face began to twitch. Martín watched, fascinated. Teo knew he was looking and turned away to hide his self-made distress. Martín, embarrassed, brought him into the conversation with a direct question.

"Why'd you choose to learn farming and sheep ranching?"

"Well, it was really my father's idea. Then, I thought it'd be an easy way to make money. Turns out it's not."

Otero rolled his eyes.

"What really interests me is cattle. That's where the money is," he added emphatically.

Martín and Otero were surprised. For the first time that evening, Teo was showing an interest in something. But cattle? Was this a hint for a job in the valley? Why bring it up now? To Teo's surprise everybody's attention was focused on him. He almost smiled and pressed on. Turning to Martín, he suddenly asked him a torrent of questions.

"You live in the valley. Is it easy to raise cattle out there? Is the grama grass as good as they say? How about water? Hear there's a good spring called Antelope. How many head will it water? Also hear there's already a big cattle operation there run by some people named Whitney. They must be pretty smart."

Martín glanced at Otero, who was equally surprised at Teo's questions. Were they triggered by his courtesy, simple curiosity, or did Teo have something else on his mind? He suspected Teo knew more than he was telling. Without a real clue as to what that might be, he downplayed cattle in his answer.

"Raising anything, in the valley or wherever, isn't easy. We raise sheep, not cattle. Mostly, I'm concerned with the flocks and crops. Watching lambs drop in the spring or seeing a good harvest come in isn't exactly exciting. But if you do a lot of the work yourself, it's sure satisfying."

"What about cattle?"

"Of course, there's cattle ranching in the valley. Cattle eat the same grass our sheep do. Not quite as closely, fortunately."

He smiled and added untruthfully, "Afraid I don't know what's going on in the cattle business out there."

Teo burst out again, this time on a totally different tack.

"You know, I really miss Albuquerque. There's not much social life around here."

It was Catalina's turn to roll her eyes.

Turning their attention to Martín, the Oteros asked about his parents, life in Manzano, crops and sheep. Of particular interest seemed to be his education. He mentioned his years at Father Ralliere's school in Tome. Otero leaned back in his chair and wiped his mouth.

"Ralliere's done a remarkable job with that school. You were fortunate to go there. I don't agree with people around here who think that education should be limited to catechism and the Bible. We Mexicans are too uneducated and narrow-minded as it is.

"He's a bit high-handed in some of his decisions. Maybe more opinionated than he should be in other matters. My father and uncle were at odds with him for years, mainly over water."

When Otero paused, Martín mentioned that before going to school he had read everything in his father's library. Asked what books he particularly liked, Martín saw Teo's facial tic start again. He guessed Teo had minimum education, read little, and thought he was either lying or exaggerating.

Supper was simple and excellent. More than enough even for Martín whose enforced fast since early morning gave him an appetite to please any hostess. He spooned up the *sopa de pollo,* chicken broth afloat with crisply fried pieces of *tortillas*, and attacked the *pozole,* a hominy and pork stew, as though his plate would be snatched off the table at any moment. Curious about its subtle flavor, he asked doña Margarita.

Pleased, she said, "We use a mild chile, *guajillo,* and a touch of the fiery *chile de arbol.*"

Dessert, freshly picked peaches and plums, answered the question as to what fruit trees grew in La Constancia's orchard. Martín drank enough of the *estancia's* light red wine to show his appreciation. Teo drank it like water. Between eating and answering questions, Martín stole glances at Catalina. She smiled every time. Teo watched and smoldered. After cups of frothy hot chocolate, Otero excused himself and Martín to lead him down the hall toward his office. Teo looked at their retreating backs and wondered what was going on.

As they walked down the long corridor, Otero said, "Unfortunately, we've done practically nothing to change this *hacienda* from the fortress it used to be into a home. We always seem to be short of time or money. Well, that's not strictly true. We did build a second floor for bedrooms over the *sala* and *comedor.*"

Midway down the hall he stopped and swung closed thick mesquite shutters folded back on either side of a deep window. Then, dropping a heavy bar in place across both of them, he looked through the peephole cut in one side.

"Here's something from our bloody past. These were last used when I was nine. Sat on the floor right here under the window. Scared to death by the noise of rifles and the shrilling of Indians."

Otero blinked his eyes and shuddered. He walked on into his office, leaned over to light the wall sconces behind his desk, and sat down. He offered Martín a thin cigar from a silver box lined with aromatic wood. Martín declined with thanks. When Otero's own cigar was drawing satisfactorily, he put elbows on the desk top and picked up the conversation exactly where Martín had left off hours earlier.

"Now, young man, if there're reasons to add to my crew at Estancia Springs, why should it be you?"

Good question, thought Martín. He had expected it and spent time thinking how he would answer.

"For twelve years I've had practical experience farming and taking care of stock."

"I can believe that."

"In addition, I've read every book I could find on breeding, raising and caring for cattle. For some reason my father has a lot of books about them, but only a few head of cattle to practice on. In the past year I've spent time studying the financial side of the business, and have a fair idea of what's happening in the cattle markets."

"I'm beginning to envy your father's library."

"It's almost indispensable. Father is pretty dedicated to sheep raising, though a number of times I've suggested we gradually switch to cattle."

And, skirting the truth, added, "So far he doesn't seem interested."

Martín underplayed his discouraging year on the north valley cattle ranch, described his stints as a lumberjack and hard rock miner.

"I should mention that my English is about as good as my Spanish."

For effect he added, "I think we're going to see more Anglo-Americans than the Whitneys running cattle in the valley."

"I'm afraid you're right. From the amount of land being sold to ranchers, there's a lot stirring about cattle."

Martín decided to bare his soul.

"To be really honest with you, don Manuel, I've spent more than enough time as my father's hired hand. Not that I haven't learned a lot from him. He's a good farmer and a great horse breeder. I may sound a little like Teo, but I want to become part of a growing cattle business."

To test him, Otero said, "What's wrong with the Whitney operation?"

"I don't know first hand. But from what I hear about the way they operate, I'd rather take a job cleaning out *acequias*."

Otero laughed. Impressed by Martín's candidness and experience, he thought for a minute.

"It's no secret we want to increase our small herd in the valley. That means more men. What kind of skills I'll need, I haven't had time to think about.

"Also, it's hardly a secret our claim to the Baca Grant is being contested by the Whitneys. In fact, I was surprised when Teo mentioned them. They may not know it yet, but when they bought the Sandoval grant, the Whitneys bought a pig in a poke. We're certain the court will find in our favor."

To show Otero he knew what was going on in the valley, Martín said, "There's certainly not enough water at Antelope Springs for five thousand head. Where're the Whitneys going next?"

"That's what worries us. They're arrogant and determined. Also moving faster than we thought they would. I'm afraid they've got their eyes on our Estancia Springs ranch. Your experience and knowledge could be really helpful to us out there. Your English, too. Jesus Chavez, my foreman, speaks none. James Whitney knows about the same amount of Spanish. I've been told he thinks all Mexicans ought to learn English but won't because they're dumb, lazy greasers."

Prophetically, he added, "This thing will work out in the long run. If you're patient, which I suppose you're not, there's probably a place for you out there. Also, could be trouble's coming to Estancia Springs. No sense sending you into it or making a commitment now I might have to take back later."

"What about Teo ?"

"He's no competition. I'd never send him out there. Why don't you spend a couple of weeks with us? I'd like to get to know you better. Maybe you feel the same way about me."

His smile and handshake confirmed the invitation. Martín had not expected the directness, simplicity and honesty in a man of Otero's power and wealth.

"We get up early at La Constancia," said Manuel, rising. "Breakfast, like supper, is at six."

At five, Martín was shaved, dressed and exploring the *hacienda* grounds. At six, along with the Oteros and Teo, he gave his full attention to *huevos revueltos,* scrambled eggs with cheese and chile, using his *tortilla* as a spoon.

At the stable, a few minutes walk from the *hacienda*, they found their horses already saddled. Manuel mounted a well-founded roan. Teo swung up onto his deep-chested bay with a white blaze on his nose and white on his right front pastern. Tall Pizarra with the rangy Martín aboard was the handsomest mount of them all. The three rode over to the stock pens where bulls were being bred. Otero was impressed by Martín's knowledgeable comments. After his initial prurient interest in bulls being mounted on cows had been satisfied, Teo became bored.

Unexpectedly, out of the open barn door raced two barking dogs chasing a rat. All three ran under the bull just being mounted. The bull, almost a thousand pounds of flesh, muscle and bone, predictably spooked, wheeled and charged. At top speed it slammed into the gate chained closed to a sturdy post, snapping the post off cleanly. The splintered gate oscillated wildly, pivoting so rapidly on its pintles that Otero, sitting his roan at the gate's hinged end, had no time nor room to move. Struck by the gate's remnants, his horse reared in terror, unseating Manuel and pitching him over the fence where he landed inside the corral hard on his shoulder and head.

Maddened by its collision with the gate, wild-eyed with fear, the bull headed for the nearest target, a group of women weaving in the shade of a cottonwood outside a nearby adobe workshop. Fortunately, Martín was still on Pizarra. He shouted at Teo to care for Manuel and instantly kicked his horse into a run in pursuit of the bull, building a loop in his rawhide *reata* as he went. In a dozen strides the long-legged gray overtook the crazed animal. Martín's big loop floated out and dropped cleanly over its head. Three quick dallies around the flat saddle horn anchored the other end of the *reata*. To prevent their being capsized, he veered horse and bull gradually away from the screaming, scattering women. Slowed, the bull stopped, then followed him docilely back to the barn.

Teo had disappeared. Semi-conscious, Otero lay on the ground face up, tended by two stockmen dabbing his face awkwardly with dripping bandanas. Martín ran from the stock well with a pail of cold water and carefully bathed Otero's forehead, neck and wrists. He could not understand Teo's disappearance. Finally Otero sat up, dazed but still able to yell furiously at his stockmen.

"What idiot left the barn doors open?" Then, "Where's Teo?"

Unable to answer either question, Martín helped Otero to his feet and onto his horse, and slowly they rode back to the *hacienda*. To their disgust, Teo was sitting in the *comedor* waiting for someone to serve him dinner.

For months Manuel's growing hostility toward his nephew had been fueled by Teo's ineptitude and lack of interest in farming and ranching.

Manuel lowered his face to within inches of Teo's, and with veins pulsing in his face roared, "You goddamned ungrateful pup. Get your things and get out of this house now! I'll talk to your father later."

Otero stalked out of the room, fists clenched at his sides. Teo's face turned red with embarrassment and anger.

As furious as Otero, but with more control in his voice, Martín said, "If you felt nothing else for don Manuel, common decency should have told you to help him."

Teo snarled, "None of your goddamned business, Wolf. After all I've done for him, this is what I get." Then lamely, "I make my own decisions. Maybe you and I better meet outside."

"You can count on it," Martín answered quietly.

While Teo went to get his few belongings, Martín walked down the *zaguan* and leaned against the baking front adobe wall. Shortly, Teo emerged with a cloth bag in his hand. He pivoted around to face Martín, yelling like an angry child.

"What makes you think you can tell me what to do and not do ? I was here first. And you better stay away from Catalina. She's in love with me."

Martín couldn't stifle his laugh. Teo's face flushed and his facial tic started pulsing again. Suddenly, he dropped the clothing bag to fumble for his belt knife.

"I'm going to cut off your *cohones*," and suddenly lunged forward.

"Stupid move," said Martín, grabbing Teo's wrist above his knife hand, twisting it clockwise. As he increased the pressure, his eyes stayed locked on Teo's until his arm gave way and he rotated it up into the middle of his back, forcing him to his knees. The knife fell to the ground. Martín released Teo's wrist and, to make his bloodless victory a bit sweeter, picked up and handed the knife to him. Without a word, the stocky figure got up and disappeared toward the stable.

The day after his accident Manuel, recovered but still bruised, said, "Let me show you La Constancia."

Their horses kicked up small puffs of dust from the bone-dry road as they rode south through the *estancia*.

"If the men are doing their jobs, I can tell by looking at the results, not by how hard they appear to be working. That's why I make this ride at least three times a week."

"Listen to that," he said, pointing to the grist mill straddling a deep, free-running *acequia madre* powering a wood water wheel that groaned loudly and constantly with every revolution.

"Now you know how La Constancia got its name. With a breeze off the river you can hear that damn thing wailing for miles. The sound never stops, but it means cheap milling for us and our neighbors so nobody complains."

"We keep only enough sheep here for breeding, to feed ourselves and the workers. Our main flocks are in the valley."

"How much do they pay for the sheep they eat?"

"Nothing. They work hard, probably deserve more than we can pay them. I grind their corn free, they take what fruit they want from the orchard. With that, the mutton, wool and hides, we get extra loyalty and practically no theft."

Makes good sense, Martín thought. Then he asked the question always in the back of his mind.

"How do you get along with the Anglo-Americans around here?"

Otero answered hesitantly. "Whether their fault or ours, not all that well. Many of them believe that God sent them out here to save us. From what, I don't know. We've saved a lot of them by teaching them dry farming and the planting of drought-resistant crops. Some of them I admire, though."

"I hope they're not like the ones I've met in the valley," said Martín. "They seem to think that land here in New Mexico is their inalienable right. Just lying around for the taking."

"Unfortunately, a lot of Anglos have that attitude. Another problem is that they don't try to understand how we think, not that it's easy. Take land, for instance. The Mexican loves it, is even courteous to it. That trait makes us seem simple, therefore vulnerable. And as you know, just below the surface in most Mexican men is that pride in masculinity — *machismo.*"

"Don't tell me about *machismo*. I learned more than I wanted to know about it in the lumber camp. Most of it added up to knife fights with me."

Manuel laughed. "Well, you know more than many of us. The essence of my belief about Mexicans is that we value life for what it *is,* Anglo-Americans for what they can *do* with it. There's an old Spanish *dicho* which you may know, *Lo que puede,*" 'What's possible is enough.' "

They rode into the *pueblito* of small adobes housing his workers. Chickens, dogs and pigs fled their horses' hooves. Many women Otero knew by name. His greetings were rewarded with smiles and bows, which he returned.

On the ride back to the *hacienda* Martín, urged on by Otero, critiqued what he had seen, asked endless questions about farming practices and equipment. Too often Otero was embarrassed to find himself answering, "We've always done it that way," no one ever having challenged whether "that way" was the best way.

On a whim next day, to eliminate the tedium of workers bringing water into the barn by the bucket, Martín built a narrow wood flume to carry it from the stock well to the barn and into a small holding tank inside. Otero thanked him. Two days later a small trough appeared, running from the well outside and into a small tank inside the kitchen. Days sped by. Tasks were assigned to Martín, with Otero overseeing less and less as his confidence in him grew.

Martín never missed a chance to meet Catalina at the little pueblo where she used her talents for healing. Sick children, pregnant mothers, injured men, almost all responded to her gentle and positive manner and herb *remedios.* One afternoon he watched squeamishly as she set and dressed a worker's badly mangled hand.

Afterward they rode through the *bosque* to the edge of the Rio Grande to watch the sun make another dramatic exit over the distant western mountains. Idly he threw a stick into the current and turned to look at Catalina.

"You're remarkable. That man smiled even though you were hurting him. How did you learn to heal and take care of people?"

She smiled shyly.

"Mother and I were on an errand to the *pueblito*. I was about fifteen. A woman, crying, approached me, not Mother, and thrust her pathetic little baby into my arms. *'Por Dios, ella salve,'* she said. The child was limp and its eyes closed. As I cuddled the poor little girl, the strangest thing happened. I felt a tingling in my arms, something like warmth and a faint vibration."

"Didn't it scare you?"

"Not really, but it startled me. I could tell that something good, yet completely natural was about to happen. There seemed to be a sort of power or strength in me I didn't know was there. Minutes later the child opened her eyes and gave me the sweetest smile. Then she drank water and ate a bit of food which she previously refused. In days she was almost well."

"What made her sick?"

"I never found out. But mothers in the *pueblito* kept asking me to look at their sick children. I could hold them, rock and maybe massage them. Most seemed to improve. Why, I don't know. It was frustrating not knowing what it was I was doing right. At the same time, wonderful that I could do it.

"A *curandera* in Tome told me I was a natural healer. 'The gift is from God,' she said. But I still knew nothing about healing. I began to spend time with her to learn about various *remedios,* when and where to pick herbs, how to wash and dry them, how to set bones and bandage wounds.

One thing led to another, so here I am pretending to practice medicine without a license, which I hear are very few in New Mexico Territory."

"What do your parents think about all this?"

"Mother thinks it's wonderful. Prays for me every Sunday at church. Father thinks I'm a little odd, but takes a practical view. He says anything that helps our workers has got to be good."

Martín looked at Catalina.

"Would you take care of me if I were sick or hurt? I don't mean a miracle, just take care of me?"

She leaned over and laid her head on his arm. "You know I would! But you better never need it!"

Their mutual affection grew, nourished by less-than-accidental touchings, searching looks, occasional words, but few outward displays. Saturday's supper was a trial for them both. Martín was leaving the next day. Catalina sighed softly and frequently, inaudibly she hoped, but heard by her parents as they noticed the glances exchanged between the two.

Supper over, Manuel again walked Martín to his office.

"You've been a most entertaining guest and a real help. It's refreshing to have another point of view about things you do the same way every day. I hope you've learned from me, too.

"The damn grant question is still wide open. I keep saying it, but hopefully the court will decide in a few weeks. And two weeks from tomorrow we're giving a *baile* to celebrate Catalina's eighteenth birthday. We'd be honored to again have you as our guest. By then, maybe there'll be two reasons to celebrate."

"Of course, I'll be here! If only for one reason."

Sunday morning breakfast was over too quickly. All three Oteros were dressed to go to mass after Martín left. He and Catalina exchanged undisguised longing glances across the table. Hands clasped, the two walked slowly down the *zaguan*, followed discreetly by the Oteros. Outside in the hot early morning sun, Pizarra, watered, fed and rubbed down, nickered a welcome. Martín scratched his nose, swung up into the saddle and, as Catalina handed up a cotton *bolsa* bulging with roast chicken and *tortillas,* he looked into her eyes.

She placed her hand gently on his leg and said, with a misty smile, *"Vaya con Dios, hasta la vista."*

Sombrero in hand, he smiled and made a sweeping bow. *"Mille gracias para todo,"* he said.

With just the suggestion of reins on his neck, Pizarra wheeled and headed toward the mountains on the long road back to his home in Manzano.

Out of sight of the *hacienda*, Martín leaned over and whispered, "See, old friend. I told you it might be worth the trip."

CHAPTER 7

FEET PROPPED on a chair, fingers laced behind his head, Joel Whitney looked out on the top floor of the city's newest and tallest office building, the eight-story, Whitney-owned headquarters of the family's thriving Back Bay Bank & Trust Company. He smiled possessively as if he owned the city and Boston Harbor, too. Opposite him on a windowsill sat his brother James, legs crossed, hands cupped on one knee.

"By God, we did it, James! We're in the cattle business! At last you can be the cowboy you've wanted to be since you were six."

He waved a telegram like a starter's flag in his brother's face.

"The confirmation of our buy of the Sandoval Grant. Only five thousand dollars!"

James, all smiles, answered prophetically, "Almost too good to be true."

"No, we're just smarter than most people, James. You're going to make that outfit into the most profitable business we've ever had. Catch the next train, and better buy some duds in Albuquerque so you won't scare those five thousand head of cattle being driven up from Texas."

Back Bay bred, Harvard educated, rich, the new would-be cattle barons and owners of the Sandoval Grant were cocky Boston "Brahmins." Political acquaintances in Santa

Fe told them not to worry about the legality in the grant, though some thought its title suspect. If they were sued, the sellers assured them, the right application of money would tilt the court in their favor. "That's the way things are done out here."

The Whitneys certainly didn't mind spending their abundant resources for important things like bribes. Excited, Joel stood up, jammed hands in his pockets and, to reassure himself, added up the pluses out loud.

"James, just look at what we've got. A bargain grant with grama grass all over it, a spring at Antelope, soon an even better one at Estancia, climbing beef prices, and the railroad coming practically into our backyard. What's to prevent us from becoming cattlemen like John Chisum or Charlie Goodnight? Not a goddamn thing! The sooner you get on that train, the better."

Putting his brother in charge of the cattle operation turned out to be a bad mistake. James knew absolutely nothing about ranching, thought there was little worth learning, and lacked his brother's shrewdness and patience. As far as James was concerned, the superiority of a Harvard education and the right application of money would solve any problems the "greasers" could bring. Much of New Mexico Territory was still open grazing land. But James was smart enough to hedge his bet. As far as he was concerned, every rancher, legitimate or otherwise, had to get off their land. To "convince" people to move, he needed muscle. On advice from friends in Santa Fe he hired a group of *Tejanos,* ex-Texas gunmen with established reputations The seven James chose had been chased out of state by the Texas Rangers some years before. With an easy move into adjacent New Mexico, they became available to the highest bidder. All but one of the group Whitney "bought" had been part of the "Rio Grande Posse," a group which earned a deserved reputation for brutality in the El Paso Salt Wars. Their first employment opportunity in New Mexico Territory came in the Lincoln County "war" of 1878.

Whitney's seven *Tejanos* had a leader of sorts, Jack Baird, chosen in recognition of his ruthless performance in Lincoln County. Born in 1848 in the Texas panhandle's tough community of Tascosa, he was only four years old when abandoned by his mother. She never knew who his father was. In effect, he became a ward of the town. Even in troubled Tascosa, Baird stood out. Tall, wiry and humorless, his blossoming proficiency with gun and knife eventually got him thrown, not without difficulty, out of town. He drifted, anywhere, convinced the world owed him something, taking life and money without a second thought.

Only one of the seven *Tejanos* had not been a part of the Rio Grande Posse. Ignored by the Texans because he was Mexican, Pecho Torres was Whitney's most controversial hire. James added him because he had a reputation for polished skills as an intimidator. When young, Torres slipped over the Rio Bravo from Coahuila into Presidio, Texas, making his way north robbing and killing frequently and efficiently. Also swept out of Texas by the Rangers, Torres appeared in Lincoln to help hold the town and county hostage. Small and black-haired, he was tolerated by his six companions out of fear. Most of his time he spent alone, watching his back.

With gunslingers much in evidence, Whitney began his methodical crusade against squatters Otero had indulged for years, throwing one after another off his land. Between Antelope and Estancia Springs was the barely productive acreage of Candido Quintana. For fifteen years Candido and his family eked out a living. All they had to show for their labor was a small two-room adobe flanked by a kitchen garden, stunted pigs, a few scrawny chickens, listless dogs and a hundred steers slowly starving to death. So rare were visitors that when he heard Whitney and his seven ride in, Candido lifted his head and smiled. The smile quickly disappeared when Whitney, leading his *Tejanos,* almost rode him down.

As if Quintana were too stupid to understand English

in a normal tone of voice, Whitney shouted, "This is my land. I want you off it by noon tomorrow."

Candido Quintana spoke English infrequently, but he knew enough to realize that the small world he and his family had so patiently built for themselves was unraveling in front of his eyes.

"But, señor, don Manuel says I can be here forever. And there is no need to speak so loud."

"Otero doesn't own this land. I do. By noon tomorrow you and your family will be off it or you'll be goddamn sorry," he shouted.

Though convinced he was in the right, Whitney had enough conscience to try to soften what he was doing. He'd seen some of Quintana's sorry cattle.

In a burst of generosity he said, "I'll buy your whole herd for five dollars a head. You can't beat that offer."

Whitney knew that even culls were selling for ten dollars a head. Candido knew it, too.

"But, señor," he started to protest.

Whitney nodded to the *Tejanos*. They formed a semi-circle around the Mexican, driving him slowly back against the wall of his adobe home and stared down at him. Jack Baird drew a pistol and almost blew the head off a passing pig. All eight rode off together, their horses' hooves destroying the kitchen garden.

Not everyone was so easily intimidated, especially those who legitimately owned their land. A stubborn Anglo-American named McAfee refused to leave Berendo, his ranch of many years near Antelope Springs. Whitney's attempt to be friendly were rebuffed, as were his threats of legal action. McAfee knew no decision had been made on the Sandoval vs. Baca claims, so there was no legal club Whitney could use. Nor was he particularly awed by the *Tejanos* sent to lean on him.

Tough as boot leather himself, McAfee had a half-dozen hands who were adept at surviving. Negotiations ended abruptly when McAfee shot and slightly wounded one of

Whitney's hard cases trying to fire the barn. Realizing his tactics had been a bit crude, Whitney sent Baird for Aaron Wolf, hoping McAfee's friend and neighbor could find some way to convince him to move out.

Spoiled by no-cost removals of squatters on the Sandoval Grant, Whitney balked when Aaron tried to talk sense to him.

"Short of killing McAfee, which I'm sure has occurred to you, the only way to get rid of him is to buy him out. Offer him what his land is really worth, what his improvements are worth. Offer to buy his cattle at market price. Pay off his hands. Offer him a bonus."

"That'll cost too damn much. What if he still won't go?"

"You want to be a rancher? It costs money, James. After you've made your offer, tell McAfee you're fencing in Antelope Springs. He'll be more inclined to sell when he knows he'll have trouble watering his stock. Of course, you won't have any friends left around here. But then, you probably don't now."

Impatient, Whitney refused to wait for the court decision on the grants. He had too many cattle and too little water. His next move would have to be onto Otero's ranch at Estancia Springs. He planned to treat Otero as just another squatter. Besides his hired guns, he had with him his brother-in-law and future ranch foreman for Estancia Springs, Arthur Bailache.

This time he would plan before acting.

CHAPTER 8

THE NEAR FATAL TRIP through the canyon shortcut dampened Martín's ardor for adventure enough to convince him to take the long way home. This meant riding around the southern tip of the Manzanos. At the end of the forty-mile trip, he rode wearily up the lane to his home, scarcely noticing the unfamiliar horse and buggy tethered in front. Stiffly, he dismounted and led leg-weary Pizarra into his stall, gave him oats, water and a cursory rubdown.

On the porch under the *portal* he took off his boots, held them in one hand while opening the door into the *sala* with the other. He stepped in to be greeted with a dark look from his father. A well-dressed man about his own age was pretending to talk to Aaron while really staring at his sister Ofelia. Aaron smiled and gestured toward his guest.

"Martín, this is James Whitney," adding superfluously, "He and his brother own the Sandoval Grant. They're running a lot of cattle at Antelope Springs. James has a job proposition for you. Didn't know when you'd be back, so I almost accepted for you."

Hesitantly, Martín took the man's offered hand. Whitney went right to the point.

"Your father said you're interested in a 'going' cattle operation. We're sure 'going'! Got five thousand head out near Antelope Springs, and we need all the *vaqueros* we can find."

"*Vaquero,*" thought Martín, is probably the only Spanish word he knows.

"Might even be a full-time job for you later on," said Whitney, trying to sweeten the offer.

Martín could not resist agitating Whitney.

"I hear the Sandoval Grant purchase is being contested by the owners of the Baca."

"D'you think we'd let some greaser claim get in the way of ours?" snapped Whitney contemptuously, instantly regretting his poor choice of words for this audience.

Ofelia pivoted and walked out of the room. Martín tensed. Even Aaron stirred restlessly, thankful his wife was not there. Whitney stood awkwardly, wishing he could take back his words.

On the verge of a sharp reply, Martín swallowed it.

Instead, he said politely, "That's an interesting offer. I'd like to think about it and talk to my father. If you'll excuse me."

Seething, he left the room, too, contrasting the man's arrogance to Otero's civility. When he was sure Whitney had left, Martín strode back into the *sala* to confront his father.

"What was that all about? You were going to accept a job for *me?* Working for a man who's part owner of a disputed land grant and calls Mexicans 'greasers' in front of your daughter and son? Guess you've already chosen sides."

Aaron flushed and countered lamely. "So, you've spent a couple of weeks with Otero at La Constancia and didn't have the stomach to tell me you were going."

Martín winced.

"Who knows," Aaron continued. "Maybe Otero's claim is the one that's no good."

Even from his father, that was all Martín could take.

"For years you've never given a damn about what *I* wanted to do, which happens to be ranching. Now all of a sudden you're claiming to be helping by wanting me to throw in with some Anglos doing high-handed ranching in the valley."

"What're you talking about? You've always had a job here when you wanted it. Pay, room and board. I fix you up with a job on a cattle ranch and now you're complaining."

"Yes. There's always been a job available here, sheep and farming. As for those Eastern cattle ranchers, you know the Whitneys are throwing people off land they've been on for generations. And those two are on land they may not even own!"

"Well, the squatters sure don't own it," Aaron replied.

Martín couldn't suppress his sarcasm.

"Why'd you think Whitney hired those *Tejanos?* To amuse himself around the campfire with their funny stories about all the people they've killed? You know as well as I do they're the muscle he's using to throw out anybody who gets in his way. What's in this deal for you? You wouldn't be pushing me so hard in their direction if there wasn't."

That was too close to the bone for Aaron. Pretending to be insulted, abruptly he turned and left the room.

To his retreating back Martín said loudly, "Otero offered me a job." Then, still short of the whole truth, in an even louder voice said, "I think I'll take it."

For the next two weeks, the Wolf family walked on eggs. Only when necessary did Ofelia and Martín speak to Aaron, and then in tense, clipped sentences. Even his relationship with Daisy seemed strained. Always the conciliator, she tried local gossip to deflect arguments or break the silence at mealtime. The others seldom spoke. Aaron drank even more.

To impatient Martín, Catalina's baile seemed months, not just days away.

"Come on!" Ofelia said, "you're acting like a love-struck sixteen-year-old. I'm sure Catalina's a marvelous girl, but you're not marrying her next week, are you? For heaven's sake, stop fidgeting. I could use some help around here, you know."

He looked at Ofelia and smiled. She tousled his hair.

"Your mind's wandering. So I've written down a list of things we need. Maybe you can spare some of your invaluable time by going to the store for me. By the way, add pencils to the list. I'm writing a story and my last pencil is too short to sharpen."

He could walk down to the general store, but it was too hot. Leisurely, he saddled Pizarra and rode him to the center of town. In front of one of the two general stores was a horse and buggy which he recognized as Whitney's, and tethered next to it a deep-chested bay with a white blaze on its nose and white on its right front pastern.

In seconds Martín remembered. It had to be Teo's horse, the one he rode at La Constancia. What was he doing in Manzano? Being reeled in by James Whitney, he guessed. Anything for money! Probably had sold out by telling Whitney what he knew of Otero's plans. Well, considering that he was waiting for the court's decision, that was more than Otero knew.

Hating Teo would be easier if he were Anglo. Instead, Martín felt sorry for him, but not sorry enough to lose a chance to worry him. He waited. After five minutes, Whitney and Teo walked out together. Whitney waved, Teo panicked, scrambling onto his horse and galloping north out of town.

Purchases made, Martín decided to drop in on Charles Kusz and bring him up to date. His office was barely a hundred yards down the road. The door was open, but Martín knocked anyway, then walked inside. Kusz was back in the clutter of his press room/kitchen filling a type stick. At the sound of footsteps he looked and smiled when he saw Martín.

"How did it go with Otero?"

"Looks pretty good. Except for the suit over the grants which is still hanging fire. Otero wants me to work for him in the valley when it's settled. Guess who I just saw in town? Teo Armijo, don Manuel's nephew. Looks like he's sold out to the Whitneys."

After hearing the story of the bull incident, Kusz was hardly surprised.

"Anything else?"

"The Oteros certainly have a nice daughter. I'm going

back to La Constancia tomorrow for her eighteenth birthday *baile*."

That was all Martín would volunteer. Kusz suppressed a smile.

Next morning Martín and Pizarra were off early for La Constancia. All he could think about was Catalina and the possibility of a job with Otero. He planned to spend the night before the *baile* in Tome so he would arrive refreshed and clean. This time he told Aaron where he was going. In return he got a disgusted look.

CHAPTER 9

PIZARRA'S GAIT seemed brisker, the miles shorter, hot weather less of a burden than the last time he went to La Constancia. When Martín reached the dirt road along the edge of the *estancia,* he turned north toward Tome. Returning from there after an errand for doña Margarita, Tranquilo Villareal hailed him.

"Hola! Buenos tardes, señor Martín. Where're you going? You're expected at the *hacienda.*"

His embarrassment at arriving a day early quickly evaporated with margarita's enthusiastic welcome as he entered the *sala.*

"We need all the help we can get!"

Even warmer was his reception from Catalina, glowing from hard work like her mother. She cupped Martín's face in her hands and kissed him on the lips with enthusiasm. One glance at the chaos of decorations strewn around the room told him that his warm reception was half affection, half relief.

Immediately pressed into service, he wobbled ineptly on chairs to fasten paper garlands and streamers in hard-to-reach places. Finally, told to just sit and entertain them, he kept them laughing with stories about growing up in Manzano.

"When I was about ten we had a bad winter drought that continued on into spring and summer. Every farmer in the area was really worried about their corn crop. My mother, a very religious woman, was a good friend of the priest who served our town and several others nearby. She talked him into carrying a statue of the Savior around the local fields while praying for rain. Well, wouldn't you know, that night we had the worst hailstorm I've ever seen. Anything that was growing was smashed flat.

"Next morning Father and I were up early to see what was left — practically nothing. But there was Mother all by herself carrying a statue of the Virgin Mary around our battered field and looking like she was talking to herself. We hurried up, and Father said, 'What do you think you're doing?'

"Without hesitation she turned and looked at us. 'What do you think I'm doing? Showing our Virgin what a terrible thing her son has done.' "

Shortly before supper on Friday the decorations were finished. The room looked beautiful. Don Manuel wisely had found important things to do elsewhere, but on Saturday morning, to Martín's relief, Otero borrowed him from the women.

Out of their hearing he said, "Despite my optimism, the court still hasn't handed down a decision. I'll bet the Whitneys feel as frustrated as I do. Don't want to keep you hanging about a job in the valley, but I also don't want to lose you. How about working for me here until the valley situation's resolved?"

Martín ducked his head with embarrassment. "Maybe you better first hear what I have to tell you."

He described meeting Whitney, his suspicion that Aaron might have some connection with him, and running into Teo with Whitney.

Another thing to like about Martín, thought Otero, his complete honesty.

Uncharacteristically, Otero said, "That young son-of-a-bitch! And on top of his walking away from my accident. I told Carlos, his father, last week. It just about killed him.

Of course, I had to tell Margarita. She wondered where he'd gone. Between you and me, I think even she'd had about enough of Teo.

"I feel sorry for your father. He's making an awful mistake. As for you, I'd trust you with my life. My offer stands. Now, the main thing for us to do tonight is to enjoy ourselves."

Carlos and his wife appeared before noon. Otero shook their hands, but without much enthusiasm. Martín wondered how this couple could produce such a son as Teo, so lacking in character.

Guests arrived all afternoon. Many were neighbors. Sleeping arrangements for those from further away had been made in Tome or in the hamlet of Adelino, a few miles north of La Constancia. The huge doors to the *zaguan* had been unbolted and swung open in welcome. All three Oteros greeted their guests at the parlor door halfway up the *zaguan*. Women were led to the *sala* where they could gossip and sip wine punch. Men were urged on to Otero's office, temporarily an abundant source of rum, tequila, aguardiente and "Pass" whiskey from Texas. More than a few wives sent their husbands back to the office to bring them stronger spirits than those being served in the *sala*.

Expecting to be surrounded by the *gente fina,* people of money, education and delicate manners, Martín instead found local farmers with calloused hands and honest, lined faces all greeted by the Oteros as friends and equals.

By six the *sala,* largest of the *hacienda* rooms, was filled. Musicians tuned up in a corner. This was Martín's first *baile*. In Manzano he had been to his share of *fandangos*. The difference between the two, he discovered, was their hosts. *Fandangos,* generally rough-and-tumble community affairs, were organized as often as an excuse could be found. A *baile* was private and more formal, supposedly given by the *gente fina*.

Musicians for either were recruited locally. Their enthusiasm made up for lack of talent. At Catalina's *baile* two violins and a guitar accompanied by a small drum called a *"tombe"* comprised the "orchestra." The group's maestro earned his job more for his ready wit than a good singing voice. His tips depended on how amused or flattered the dancing couples were by his improvised verses. Introductions between dancers weren't needed. Most knew each other, or a beckoning glance and smile at a prospective partner was enough.

"Primero la misa, despues la mesa," goes an old Spanish *dicho.* "First the mass, then the table." This night the *dicho* was reversed. The Church forgave drinking, practically any indiscretion, as long as the transgressors went to mass on Sunday. Father Ralliere's church in Tome would be packed in the morning.

Competition for dancing with Catalina at her *baile,* on her birthday, was keen. No one was younger or prettier. Martín had eyes only for her. And though she danced with many, hers always searched for him. At one point she approached him, hands behind her back, mischief in her eye. Reaching up, she cracked an egg filled with rosewater over his head. Startled, he dabbed at his hair ineffectually with his handkerchief, then laughed when he saw the same being done all over the *sala,* a sign of special affection for the victim.

Promptly at midnight the music stopped; time for more liquid refreshments, which nobody needed, and dinner, which everybody did. Doors to the *comedor* opened wide. Cloth-covered trestle tables were freighted with every delicacy La Constancia could provide. Etched glass chimneys of wall-mounted kerosene sconces threw soft, complex designs on the tablecloths, tile floor, and whitewashed walls. In tall silver candelabras candle flames swayed with the passage of guests parading past the tables of food.

Now hungry, the dancers were led to this bounty by Martín and Catalina who picked up plates, toured and tasted. They fed each other *chicharrones,* cracklings scattered around the pit-broiled lamb. Nearby rested a roast of beef, a barbecued kid, *cabrito,* and a beautifully grilled flight of chickens. Mince meat in pastry, *empanaditas,* had almost disappeared before the two got to them. Guests piled their plates with chile-laced *frijoles,* steaming *tortillas* and fresh *tamales.* At the dessert table Catalina and Martín gorged on delicate cookies called *bizcochitos* temptingly nestled among candied fruits, cakes, sugared apple pies and sweetened, stewed fruits. He poured cups of frothy hot chocolate for both of them. They then shared a single glass of *mistela,* spiced brandy punch, served warm from a beaten silver bowl, a handsome family heirloom. The deceptively strong punch was flavored with *chimaja* leaves.

Smiling at the pleasure of Catalina and her guests, the Oteros watched while standing against a nearby wall. As Martín turned to give them a smile of appreciation, Tranquilo approached Manuel and whispered to him. Otero's face changed from pleasure to startled disbelief. He made a quiet excuse to his wife who was too pleased and distracted to notice his absence. Tranquilo unobtrusively followed him out of the *sala.*

Alarmed by Otero's expression, Martín slipped from Catalina's side with an excuse and followed the two men into the cross-hall, then down the hall toward Manuel's office, where Carlos Armijo stood with an exhausted, dust-covered rider. He handed Otero a note from Jesus Chavez, Otero's Estancia Springs foreman, then slumped against the wall from fatigue. Otero had the presence of mind to pour him some brandy. Reading the note, he massaged his reddening face, rolled his eyes up as if seeking divine guidance, then raised clenched fists in fury and frustration.

"Goddamned animals!" he exploded. "Whitney's taken over our Estancia Springs ranch. He and his *Tejanos* just walked in — at gunpoint, naturally. Says we're squatters. Chavez and his men were driven off. That man has no writ, no court decision, nothing!

"Tranquilo, ride to Belen and telegraph Ernesto Henriquez, my brother-in-law in Las Vegas. Tell him to meet us in Tajique tomorrow afternoon and why we're going to need him. Carlos, you've got to help me face down Whitney."

Armijo blanched, wondering how big a price he would have to pay for owning one-third of the Baca Grant.

He hesitated a moment, then said, "I'll go tell my wife, then get my things."

Thinking out loud, Otero added, "Ernesto can catch the nine o'clock to Albuquerque, rent horses there. He'll be in Tajique by late afternoon. I also want you to take a note to the sheriff in Belen. If he's there, he can follow us with a posse. Wait a moment, Tranquilo, I'll write out both the note and telegram."

At his desk which had served as a makeshift bar, Otero sent the liquor bottles crashing to the floor with a sweep of his hand. In the cleared space he hastily scribbled out a wire to his brother-in-law and a note to the sheriff.

Martín thought through the current crisis. A commitment to Otero now could reap benefits later. Manuel would not forget. What the risks were, Martín didn't know. But sixty miles from the Estancia Springs they didn't seem all that great. He stood quietly in front of the desk until Otero finished the notes and looked up.

"Well?"

"I'm coming with you."

"Don't be a goddamn fool. Thank you anyway. You don't even work for me yet. What happens at Estancia Springs isn't your concern or responsibility."

"I know, I know. Besides showing you a shortcut through the Manzanos to Tajique, there are other ways I can help."

Otero calmed down. He leaned back in his chair and looked Martín over thoughtfully, liking his determination and knowing this steady young man would add needed weight to his too-small party. He guessed at least ten made up the Whitney group. Was it fair to include Martín?

The odds were bad, the situation a gamble at best. A bit desperate, Otero made up his mind. From the desk drawer he dug out a key, pivoted around and unlocked the gun cabinet behind him. He turned back to face Martín.

"What can I arm you with?"

"Nothing, thank you. I've got a Winchester in my saddle boot."

Otero shook his head in doubt, and from a drawer under neatly aligned gun butts pulled two Colt .44 revolvers. He fished out a box of shells and loaded both weapons, careful not to put a live round under their hammers. One Colt he thrust in his waistband, the other, with extra shells for both, into his coat pocket.

As he rose, Otero said rather formally to Martín, Tranquilo and the exhausted rider, "If you'll excuse me, I must find my wife and daughter."

As inconspicuously as possible, Otero found and steered them out of the *sala* into the hall. Calmly he explained what had happened at Estancia Springs and what had to be done.

For weeks premonitions of this moment had haunted Margarita. Now she hid her face in her hands. Kindly, and with a small smile, he raised her chin, put his arm around Catalina, and tried to convince them that the problem was simply a legal matter that could be settled without violence. Both knew better.

Catalina squared her shoulders.

"Mother, go back to our guests. I'll make arrangements in the kitchen for provisions."

Few were aware that anything was wrong. Music started again, and couples began drifting back into the *sala*.

Shortly after one o'clock in the morning the sleepy stable *mozo* was shaken awake and told to bring up a string of mounts: two for each of the party but only one of them saddled, and two fresh horses for the vaquero from the Springs who, despite his exhaustion, was determined to return with Otero.

Catalina appeared with food for five packed in cloth bags tied with rawhide strips with which to lash them to the saddle horns. Carlos came out of the *zaguan* entrance, obviously nervous, then mounted and fidgeted in his saddle. The exhausted valley rider slumped on his horse, asleep.

As Martín stepped out of the passageway, Catalina drew him into the shadows of the huge gates. She crossed herself and whispered, *"Vaya con Dios,"* as she kissed him, first on the cheek, then firmly on the mouth. They clung together, but quickly separated as Otero emerged from the *zaguan* looking grim, noticing nothing. He glanced impassively at Carlos, grimaced, reined his horse sharply around, and with his spurs kicked him into a fast walk.

"Andale, pues," he said.

CHAPTER 10

"DAMN, how that dead man can still haunt me!" Aaron Wolf sat straight up in his bed, hung over, his wife still asleep by his side. Another nightmare about his father was haunting his sleep. In his dream he had been an oversized fourteen again thinking about killing his father, a deep-seated wish never fulfilled. Asleep or awake, Aaron hated even the thought of him, the abusive, alcoholic, itinerant preacher. Soundlessly, he slipped out of bed, put on a jacket, tiptoed through the *sala* and out under the front *portal*. Cool mist of early morning began to clear his head. God! What a mess I've made of things, he thought as he sat down. I'm in deep with Whitney and drinking too much. Maybe it's my father's blood.

The despised image of the man floated in front of Aaron. His father, an itinerant preacher, with his wife and Aaron wandered into Kansas City, Missouri where he successfully proselytized a flock of like-minded zealots. Their belief in the preacher nourished his ego, but provided little to quiet his wife's and son's hunger. For inspiration and to forget what he was doing to his family, he turned from the Bible to the bottle in earnest. He began beating both wife and son. Aaron's mother searched for biblical pieties to rationalize their predicament and her husband's alcoholism. Young Aaron, obsessed with the idea of killing his father, looked for a way to quit the family permanently.

Propped against a post supporting the *portal* roof, knees tight against his chest for warmth, Aaron relished the memory of escape from his parents. He answered an advertisement placed by Caleb Meriwether, a farmer from southern Missouri wanting an apprentice to work with him. Aaron faked his parents' consent and made his way to Meriwether's farm. Looking back on it, the whole thing had been a risk, but he had been desperate.

What an inspiration Meriwether turned out to be! To him everything seemed possible. Any new idea promising a better yield or breed, he would try.

If it didn't work, he'd say, "Failure is learning, too."

Meriwether and young Aaron, teacher and willing student, suited each other well. Sprung from the smothering snare of his parents' aggressive piety, Aaron knew he could learn quickly and, in gratitude, worked hard.

Widowed, never remarried, Meriwether indulged himself in breeding fine horses and hunting. Both interests and skills he passed on to Aaron. He also loved to read. The two spent most evenings by kerosene lamps until their eyes refused more words. Aaron's curiosity soon outstripped Meriwether's ability to tutor his apprentice. Sent by Caleb to the only school in that rural area, Aaron quickly soaked up its small store of knowledge.

Eight mutually beneficial years with Caleb proved long enough for both. Headlines in the local paper, "WAR WITH MEXICO," gave Aaron an inarguable excuse to leave.

Considering where volunteering for the Army eventually led him, thought Aaron, that decision was the smartest he ever made. Recognizing his talents, the Army assigned him as chief hunter and scout for the regiment raised and led by Colonel Alexander Doniphan. The six-and-a-half-foot, two-hundred-forty-pound, red-headed Irish lawyer from Liberty, Missouri recruited mostly frontiersmen. Even in that select company, Aaron distinguished himself as the column marched west to join General Stephen Kearney who had conquered Spanish-held New Mexico territory.

Aaron could find game in country others would swear was barren. In an empty landscape he unerringly sensed the presence of Indians. On reaching Santa Fe, his reputation had grown to the point that the local garrison virtually kidnapped him so he could scout for them. The Santa Fe detachment was a lot more concerned about raids by the Navajo, Ute, Apache and Comanche than warring with Mexico.

In the middle of a New Mexican winter and in its wisdom, the Santa Fe garrison decided it was necessary for a small survey party to explore the Estancia Valley area. Aaron was assigned to lead it. Below Albuquerque, through Cañon de Infierno the party labored east through snow and, despite the canyon's name, almost froze to death before entering the equally cold Estancia Valley, then virtually unknown to Americans. One of the party's main assignments was to explore the valley and count noses of friendly Pueblo Indians. If they ran into Apache or Comanche, they were to count them, too, but from a distance.

Exiting Cañon Infierno near Chilili, Aaron led the party south through the small towns of Tajique, Torreon, and on to Manzano. There they stopped to rest, resupply and feed their mounts on local grass which they cleared of snow.

Manzano's *alcalde,* who combined the office of mayor and village *mayordomo,* invited the small army group to a rare winter *fandango,* their arrival providing all the excuse needed. Not even in Santa Fe, where *fandangos* were held at the drop of a *sombrero,* had Aaron seen such wild abandon. The floor of the parish hall next to the church was filled with dancing couples, their enthusiasm undampened by off-key voices, poorly tuned violins and guitars. As each dance ended, the alcalde and his wife, a bottle in her plump hand, judged which couple appeared most graceful and treated the pair to a swallow of *aguardiente.*

Adjacent to the dancing was another room serving as a makeshift bar. Aaron wandered in and discovered the *fandango's* second most popular activity. Just as he stepped through the door, a knife-wielding drunk caromed off a wall into Aaron, sliding unconscious to the floor. In progress around him were fist and knife fights between men whose women had been danced with without permission, or who felt their honor somehow impugned. More sober guests were throwing the fighters bodily out of the building.

To Aaron's surprise, as many women smoked as did men, gracefully shaking black tobacco from a small flask, a *guajito,* into the *hoja,* a cornhusk wrapper. He tried one but found the combination too heady for his tobacco chewing tastes.

Deseidero Herrera was one of the few young women at the dance who did not smoke. The pretty girl was brushing damp hair back from her face after a wild turn on the floor when Aaron literally bumped into her. Unable to excuse himself politely in his limited Spanish, by way of introduction he bowed stiffly with a smile and away they danced, often and well. Barely seventeen, Deseidero had a radiant manner and maturity that bewitched Aaron then and still did, thirty-five years later.

His shaky Spanish fumbled her first name. To her delight he shortened it on the spot to "Daisy." Despite the lack of a mutual language, their relationship flourished. When the small Army column moved south oust of Manzano, Aaron pulled Daisy close and promised to return. And when given leave, he did.

Like most women in Manzano, as well as in the rest of New Mexico Territory, Daisy was illiterate and also, like most Mexicans, a quick learner. During the weeks of his leave Aaron taught Daisy how to speak, read, write basic English and do simple sums. In turn she taught him to speak acceptable Spanish. Each day his fascination with her grew.

Aaron's interest in Daisy was not diminished by her widowed mother's five-thousand-acre *sitio*. Granted to her husband for military services to Mexico, the land was almost exhausted from overplanting. It lay in the valley, north and east of Manzano. Crops were lean and the land's sparse grama grass barely supported a thousand sheep. Two elderly herders working *al partido,* a share of the flock's increase, tended them. During his leave Aaron did badly needed maintenance on farm buildings and fences. Daisy's mother did everything possible to promote the match, even offering to deed Aaron the *sitio* if he would marry Daisy and allow her to live with them until she died. In the Mexican fashion, through Daisy's mother, he soon proposed marriage, an offer which her mother and Daisy both quickly accepted as he did the *sitio.*

Mustered out of the Army in the spring of 1848, Aaron threw all his energy, talent and experience into rebuilding the productivity of the rundown acreage. His Missouri experience enabled him to coax more yield from the soil than the effort he put into it. Jealous neighbors at first called him *un hombre feliz,* a lucky man. Then they began to recognize his success for what it was: skill, yes, but mostly hard work.

A hoof kicking against the side of a stall broke into Aaron's reveries. He walked over to the stable, leaned on its half-gate and gazed at the dim shapes of his beloved horses. Every Mexican he knew loved horses, too, as much as they admired skillful horsemanship. Aaron made breeding horses seem effortless. For years he mated valley stallions, hardy, small and rough-looking, to thoroughbred mares bought in Santa Fe. Their colts paid him back many times over. Hands taller, longer-legged and necked than local stock, Aaron's glossy-coated horseflesh had the endurance of valley mounts, combined with exceptional speed. Mexicans and Anglos everywhere sought him out to trade, barter, sell, or to just learn how he produced such stock.

Shivering, Aaron ambled back from the barn to the *portal,* wondering how the first twelve years of their marriage could have been shadowed by lack of children. His fault or Daisy's? Maybe neither. Pregnancy seemed to be as natural as breathing in the valley. For years Aaron, Daisy and the town wondered what was wrong. To a collective sigh of relief, Martín was born, followed by Ofelia.

Early dawn thinned the mist but did little to relieve the chill. Quietly, he went back inside.

In a sleepy voice Daisy said, "Where've you been?" She had missed his warm bulk beside her. He sat on the bed without answering, worrying about losing touch with his son because of the Whitney business.

What a stupid mistake to have tried to sell him on working for their operation! The alternative, obviously, was to give Martín a freer hand in running the *sitio*. But that meant major changes in his own life which he was not ready to make. And maybe it was too late to retrieve Martín's interest and trust. Or let Martín chart his own course? Wasn't he already doing that? What else could Aaron do? He postponed thinking about the problem. Instead, he turned to Daisy, still half asleep.

"How'd you like to buy a new dress in Albuquerque? While you're shopping, I'll look for books."

"What a lovely idea. We could spend the night in Buffalo Spring with the Fermins. Then stay several nights in Albuquerque with the Jaramillos. We haven't seen any of them forever. Maybe Ofelia would like to come with us instead of being left here alone."

To her father's relief, Ofelia declined.

"Mother, they're several books I really want to finish, and frankly, I can clean your bedroom better when you're gone."

Unsaid was that she wanted as little contact with her father as possible. Impatiently, she listened to an unnecessary lecture on locking up the house at night.

With a durable horse hitched to their well-sprung buckboard, Aaron and Daisy drove down the lane, then north on the road toward Buffalo Spring.

CHAPTER 11

BY EARLY AFTERNOON Ofelia had scrubbed the kitchen with lye soap, broomed floors throughout the house with a special effort in her parents' room. Friendly, eager Felita shared Ofelia's outdoor lunch, then watched as she went to the barn to pull fresh hay into each manger, slop the pigs and feed the chickens. The long July twilight was ideal for reading. In a chair leaning back against the wall under the *portal,* Ofelia read and absent-mindedly scratched Felita's back with her foot.

Home education was one of several obstacles to Ofelia's making close girl friends. Her contemporaries felt inferior and jealous because they would never learn to read, write or do sums. A mixed heritage made it difficult to accept Ofelia as either a Mexican or Anglo-American.

Because Aaron was successful as a horse breeder and farmer, she was marked as the daughter of a *rico* in an area where poverty was the norm. That everyone in her family worked hard made no difference. Young Mexican men of her age she found physically attractive at first, but boring in the long run.

Confused by the attitude of her friends, she turned to her parents for advice.

"What's wrong with me? People treat me as if I'm different from them."

"You're a lovely, smart young woman which is sure to

make people jealous."

Her mother was partly right. Aaron was even closer to the truth.

"You're also paying the price for having two good heritages instead of one, and an education which few young women have."

Reading under the *portal* became too difficult in the failing afternoon light. Felita looked up expectantly as Ofelia moved her chair into the *sala*. She let the dog in, a treat forbidden when her parents were home. After gobbling table scraps from Ofelia's supper, Felita lay contentedly on the floor while her mistress read.

As she prepared for bed, Felita growled, almost always a sign of someone in their lane. This late at night? Maybe her parents were returning. Concerned, she blew out the *sala* lights and stepped out under the *portal*. Crouched between her feet, Felita continued to growl. Ofelia saw nothing, but then heard the sound of hooves. It had to be a rider on the road through town. She knew sounds were louder in the night air. She bolted the door and went to bed, a bit ill at ease.

Morning sunlight filtering through the cottonwoods and aspens around the house dissipated her concerns of the night before. With the house empty, this was a good time to wash her hair in the *acequia*. She slipped off her blouse, camisole and skirt and, dressed only in cotton pantalettes, walked into the kitchen garden to where the *acequia* ran deepest. Several times she soaped and rinsed her long hair, letting it drift in the cool, clear water. The warming sun felt delicious on her body.

Felita, in front of the house, began barking furiously. Snapping up her dripping head in concern, she heard the sound of a blow, a howl of pain, then nothing.

Moments later two strange men walked leisurely around the corner of the house up to the kitchen garden fence. Leaning on it, one foot on the lowest rail, they stared at her body.

Quickly, she folded her arms to cover her breasts, then fear made her shake violently.

"Go away!" she screamed in terror. "What do you want?"

In silence, the two clambered through the fence rails and stalked slowly toward her. She tried to jump across the *acequia*, but slipped on its muddy bank and floundered in deep water. The taller of the two waded in, grabbed her long hair roughly, dragged her dripping, thrashing body toward the stable like a side of beef. On the way he fondled her naked breasts and laughed.

Panting from the effort of dragging, holding her by the hair, Jack Baird said, "Thanks for getting ondressed. Gotta say you're the best-looking greaser gal I seen in this stinkin' town. Betcha don' get much action here. We gonna fix that."

She made no sound. To ease the pain in her scalp, she grabbed Baird by the wrist and twisted frantically to get loose. Startled by her unexpected strength, he momentarily lost his grip while pulling her into an empty stall. She looked wildly for the pitchfork that should be hanging from a post, then remembered she had left it in the corner of the stable. Instead, from a nail on the same post hung a Mexican spur with a large, sharp rowel. She snatched it off and lunged for Baird's face. Rafe Corcoran, watching the unequal struggle with amusement, quickly stepped in, threw his arm around her throat and ripped the spur from her hand.

She stood, tearless, breasts heaving, knowing the worst was to come. Baird swung hard at her face, breaking and bloodying her nose. Then he stripped her naked.

"Don't ruin the bitch, Jack. Let's do what we come for and get outta here."

Horses slammed nervously against the sides of their stalls as Baird roughly threw her down onto the hay. Pants unbuttoned, he stepped out of them and massaged his penis erect while leering at her. With his feet he spread her legs and fell heavily on her. Calloused hands kneaded her breasts while he slammed his groin against hers. Baird stank. He reeked of sweat, urine and shit. His breath was as foul as the rest of him. Despite her twisting resistance, he forced his way into her as she screamed with pain. In a minute it was over.

He withdrew, leered at her naked body and said, "Next time ah'll like it more and so will you. Yo turn, Rave."

Ofelia tried to focus glazed eyes on her new attacker. Corcoran, pants dropped but not off, had effectively immobilized himself. As he leaned over, she lashed out with both feet, catching him hard in the crotch. Holding himself, he gasped and fell doubled over with pain. Baird swung at Ofelia's face with a stinging backhand, leaving a closing and bleeding eye. Still clutching himself, Corcoran mounted his horse with difficulty.

Ofelia rolled over to burrow her face in the comforting hay. Badly bruised, blood was still running from between her legs, her nose and eye. She rose to her knees, then unsteadily to her feet, and limped to the *acequia* where, as best she could, washed the blood and filth from her body. Blood seemed to be everywhere. To ease the pain, she held herself. Cold water at first soothed, then made her shake. She staggered into the house with the clothes she gathered up by the *acequia*, then crawled into bed, forgetting to bolt the doors. Disgusted, fury and hate burning in her throat like bile, hurting physically and emotionally, Ofelia's courage finally broke. She sobbed herself into a fitful sleep.

Neighbors wanting to trade shucked corn for wheat stopped at the house to see Aaron. One look at Felita's crumpled body told them something was terribly wrong. The *sala* door was partially open. Ofelia was deep asleep in her bed, face caked with blood. One man rode swiftly for his wife while the other tried to bathe Ofelia's face. She recoiled in terror until she recognized him. With effort she remembered where her parents would be in Albuquerque. Shortly, the first neighbor returned with his wife, a motherly woman who had known Ofelia for years. She took charge as the two men hurried to telegraph Aaron and the sheriff.

CHAPTER 12

ONLY MARTÍN KNEW the Indian trail over the Manzanos. He took the lead as Otero's party moved on the first leg of its trip to the Estancia Springs ranch. With meager assistance from a waning moon, they pushed hard to quickly cross the twenty miles of nearly empty plain between La Constancia and the mouth of Cañon de Abo. Even on fresh horses, Otero, Armijo and the weary messenger half-asleep in his saddle could barely keep up with Martín's long-legged gray. Each deep in their own thoughts, they rarely spoke.

Nothing but stars showed overhead. Martín, encouraged by the good weather, decided to risk the shortcut. A clear dawn confirmed his choice, so the small party plunged into the canyon toward the steep Indian trail ahead. Rope-led second mounts slowed progress, as did rubble on the canyon floor left by the flash flood weeks earlier. Abo Springs was a logical place to breakfast, rest, water the horses and switch to fresh mounts. By eight they were at the spring. Picketed on long ropes, the horses had plenty of grazing room. Hot coffee to wash down cold *tortillas* served as breakfast.

In an hour impatient Otero rose and said, *"Vamonos!"*

After watering their horses again, they saddled fresh mounts. Up the faint, worn Indian trail in Cañon Espinosa they started. Even in daylight the indistinct path winding upward and northeast was hard to follow. Martín wondered how he had managed to descend in the near dark. Vertically, the ascent was about a thousand feet and from the top an easy few miles to Punta del Agua. Martín shunned Quarai, did not even mention it, still unsure where it fit into the ominous pattern of events in the valley.

Tajique, where they were to meet Otero's brother-in-law, Dr. Ernesto Henriquez, was eighteen miles north of Manzano on the dirt road from Punta del Agua. They arrived hours ahead of the doctor. After almost twenty-four hours continuously in the saddle, the rider from Estancia Springs rolled off his horse in exhaustion to sleep where he fell. The rest, trail-weary, too, first took care of their horses. After cold chicken, *tortillas* and the pie, all packed by Catalina, not even coffee could keep them awake. In the afternoon shadow of the Tajique church they feel asleep instantly.

* * * * *

It was said that when gunfire couldn't be heard in Las Vegas, New Mexico, the residents missed it. For Ernesto Henriquez, charter member of the local Committee of Vigilance and a doctor, gunfire meant peril as well as opportunity. Of necessity, he became an expert on shooting and on gunshot and knife wounds. His only medical competition in town was a seventy-five-year-old obstetrician.

Las Vegas' reputation as New Mexico's capitol of crime and sin crested along with the arrival of the railroad in 1879, the same year Henriquez began his practice there. In tribute to its countless bars, the town became known as "Elbow City." Some of the worst cutthroats in the Territory informally headquartered themselves at the Imperial Saloon in Old Town, the original heart of the city. The Imperial, to which Henriquez often went in a professional capacity to make "repairs," looked onto Church Street, renamed "Sodomia" Street because of its numberless whorehouses and bars.

It was rumored that Henriquez jointed the vigilantes so he could profit from casualties on both sides of a shoot-out. Whether attracted by civic duty or greed, as the result of his membership he became a deadly and fearless shot. Never hit in a gun battle, he was either lucky or treasured equally by the lawful and lawless. Well-muscled, of medium height, Henriquez's black, wavy hair hung like a thatch over dark, piercing, restless eyes. In 1878 he met and married Manuel Otero's sister. On the deaths of Manuel's father and uncle, Henriquez became a one-third owner of the Baca Grant.

* * * * *

As the sun crept over the west side of the Manzanos, Henriquez, tired and dust-covered, leading a second horse, rode into Tajique. The Otero party was asleep. He toed awake bleary-eyed Manuel. The others gradually sat up, massaged their faces and rose stiffly. After a silent appraisal of Martín from a distance, he was introduced. In his take-charge fashion, Henriquez suggested that the rider from Estancia Springs start a fire and boil water for coffee.

"We have a job to do, eh, Manuel?"

Relish showed in Ernesto's restless eyes. It was clear he looked forward to confronting Whitney.

"Hey, Carlos, where's Teo? Shouldn't he be here?"

Armijo looked away in acute embarrassment. Attention fortunately turned to hot coffee and the remains of the food packed at La Constancia.

With his mouth full Henriquez mumbled, "Manuel, tell me everything I should know about what's going on."

"Sounds a bit stupid, Ernesto, but I don't have much more information than you do. We all know that Whitney's finally figured out there's not enough water at Antelope Springs for his herd. They've split it and walked into Estancia Springs with half the herd just like they owned the place. Sons-of-bitches couldn't wait for a decision by the court!"

"Let's go in and make the decision for them!"

Ignoring Henriquez's aggressive remark, Otero continued. "With those seven *Tejanos* he hired, Whitney chased off our hands and took over the bunkhouse. So, goddamn him, there he sits like a spider waiting for us to show and do something about it. I say let's walk in and challenge his right to possession on legal grounds. He knows damn well he has no right to be there."

Otero's dim hope was that if confronted with legal realities, Whitney and his crew would move out.

Like the man, Henriquez's plan was aggressive and certainly read Whitney's character more realistically than did Otero's.

"Manuel, that just isn't going to work. Whitney's a hothead. We can't reason with him. Let's just walk in and throw the bastards out. If we move fast enough, those *Tejanos* won't know what happened. They want pay, not a gunfight. Besides there're ranchers all over the area who'd come running for a chance to get rid of him and his crew. Those gunslingers know it, too."

"Don't know how loyal they'd be, Ernesto, but we just can't ignore seven armed men."

Carlos Armijo, least aggressive of the three, expressed no opinion, but nervously exhaled a breath of concern. Nor did his brothers-in-law expect him to offer one.

The doctor rose and walked over to where Martín sat idly counting shells in his cartridge box. Henriquez looked at the Winchester in its saddle scabbard. To get his attention, with a smile on his face he carefully moved the cartridge box with a boot. Martín looked up, wondering what this was about.

Henriquez nodded in the direction of the rifle.

"Is that all you carry, Martín? No pistol?"

"Don't like them, Doctor. I hunt. Ever since I was small. Can't remember when I came home empty-handed. Couldn't afford to waste shells."

His direct, quiet manner impressed the doctor. Manuel would not have brought him along if he lacked confidence in him. Henriquez grunted something unintelligible, turned to leave, then turned back.

"Seven *pistoleros* is a lot for one rifleman to handle. But if you could find a way to keep them for interrupting our conversation with Mr. Whitney, it would be very helpful."

"I'll do my best," Martín said, looking the doctor straight in the eye.

Still uneasy, Henriquez knew talk would not improve the realities of the situation. From his saddle he unlashed a bedroll and spread it out near the church wall.

For the first time Martín started to worry about his commitment to Otero. Promising was easy, and anything seemed possible when he was at La Constancia. Now he was on the eve of trying to keep seven professional gunmen at bay, alone.

Henriquez's head bobbed up to again try to change Otero's mind about his strategy at Estancia Springs. He made no progress. Throwing hands in the air in frustration, he withdrew his head into the blankets, resigned to do it Otero's way. Fitful sleep was everyone's ration that night. Each was imagining his role for the next day.

Daybreak signaled no relief from the heat. After coffee and what remained of the *tortillas,* the five saddled their fresher mounts. Otero led them unhurriedly toward Estancia Springs thirteen miles further out in the valley. Heat from the climbing sun began its daily baking of the valley floor. Waves of it enveloped them. As if in a house of mirrors, ordinary objects at almost any distance were distorted into unreal, undulating shapes. For a mission requiring a cool head and tact, the day couldn't be worse.

Martín watched the three principals closely. Armijo was bent over the saddle horn, concern lining his face, obviously loathe to be a part of this venture. In contrast, Otero rode erect, lips compressed into a straight line, face frozen with determination. Henriquez showed nothing, body rolling easily with his horse's gait. As during the evening before, he gave every appearance of looking forward to the confrontation. Martín envied his self-confidence.

About ten in the morning the profile of the ranch's small bunkhouse and stock pens broke the horizon. In another fifteen minutes Martín could see the shimmering surface of the shallow lake supplied by an acquifer flowing out from Manzano mountain runoff. The small body of water was ringed with scrub willows and cottonwoods crowded with several thousand head of cattle.

No longer would the local ranchers be able to water their cattle as they had when Otero held Estancia Springs. Without time to fence the pond in, Whitney posted his ranch hands and the seven *Tejanos* so as to deny water to any non-Whitney stock.

Two miles before his group reached the ranch, Jesus Chavez, Otero's foreman, appeared from nowhere. *Sombrero* in hand, he said, "It's not good, don Manuel. Too many of them. Let me go with you."

"I'll remember your courageous offer, Jesus. This is simply a legal matter that my *compañeros* and I can handle."

Jesus kept the exhausted messenger with him. After a brief consultation with his brothers-in-law, without another word Otero rode straight to the bunkhouse.

CHAPTER 13

AS THE THREE RODE toward the one-room shanty, gunmen posted around the lake, apparently coached, also drifted in that direction. The only door into the cabin was on the east side of the bunkhouse under a *portal* covering a rough plank porch. The overhanging *portal* provided minimal relief from the morning sun, but on long afternoons a slightly cooler place to sit. Tethered horses already filled the short hitchrail on one side of the shack. Manuel's group rode to the nearest cattle pen where they could wrap their reins around its top rail, dismounted and strolled toward the small building. Neither Otero nor Henriquez wore holsters. Revolvers were shoved into their waistbands. Armijo was unarmed.

As the Otero party showed up, in complete silence Whitney's seven *Tejanos* also rode in, planning to surround the cabin on foot. They too found the cabin hitchrail full. Forced to retreat to the nearby cattle pen to hitch their mounts, conveniently they grouped together. For a moment the gunmen stood there, sizing up what risk the Otero trio offered. The silent consensus was that it was minimal. Paying no attention to the *Tejanos,* the three stepped up onto the plank porch, concentrating on what lay ahead.

Last to arrive at the cattle pen, Martín was virtually ignored by the gunmen. In a group the *Tejanos* ambled slowly over toward the bunkhouse. Before they could get there,

Martín dismounted, slid out his Winchester and walked ahead of the gunmen to the porch side of the shack. Into his rifle's chamber he levered a shell with a clash loud enough to be heard by the seven, then eased down the hammer. Only then was he noticed. Like dogs uncertain of each other's intentions, their eyes tracked Martín warily while he eyed them back. Rifle cradled in his left arm, right thumb on the hammer, he stood in front of the *portal*, legs apart. As if choreographed, the seven sidled between him and the cabin, to keep him out, he supposed. Some sat, others leaned against the wall. All struck what were meant to be casual, yet menacing poses. The scorching morning sun was directly in their eyes when the seven looked up at Martín.

Mouth dry, he drew a deep breath, hoping he could speak without showing his nervousness.

"The affair inside the cabin is not our concern. No one gets involved in any way, no matter what. *Comprende?*"

Jack Baird, their self-appointed leader, adjusted his gunbelt and smirked.

"You gotta be Martín Wolf. Well, Martín, there's no way yore goin' to drop us all with that there rifle. Who d'ya think yore foolin'?"

The group laughed, especially Rafe Corcoran. Baird spoke the truth. Martín was no gunfighter, but he had a gunfighter's instincts and a strong wish to stay alive. As he cocked the hammer, he pointed the rifle at Baird's midsection.

"You're right. But if anyone makes a move anywhere, for certain you'll be the first to get killed. Most likely, one or two others."

They watched with fascination as his finger softly wrapped around the trigger. Baird figured him as just another greaser lacking the resolve to shoot. Almost imperceptibly he nodded to Corcoran, nearest to the corner of the cabin. Rafe understood. Circle the cabin and get the drop on Martín from the other side. Martín also noticed the minute signal. Before Corcoran took a step, without the appearance of being aimed, the rifle fired. Baird fell heavily, the heel shot off his right boot. Martín chambered another round so quickly the sound of the first had hardly died away. All tensed, but neither a move nor sound came from any of them. With effort the chastened Baird picked himself up and brushed off the dust.

"For Christ's sake, Martín, ya coulda killed me."

"Maybe I should have. All of you sit down."

First to sit was a man who looked Mexican. Earlier, Martín noticed, the man kept apart from the group. He looked at Martín out of the corner of his eye with the hint of a smile. The rest sat or hunkered on their heels under the *portal*, making it difficult for any to quickly unholster a pistol. The burning sun in their eyes was worth the discomfort, he figured. Sweat pouring down his face, back and inside his arms, he cradled the Winchester while looking down on the seven.

Otero, Henriquez and Armijo had disappeared into the bunkhouse, a flat-roofed, adobe line shack. It was just large enough for Jesus Chavez's small crew of sheep herders who spent most of their nights out with the flocks. Fifteen feet square, the simple log and adobe cabin had two sets of over-and-under bunks. Near a third wall was a small stove for cooking and winter heat. Other furnishings were a table, two stools and a bench. Unglazed windows with rolled-up hide flaps looked to the west and east, the latter window next to a door sagging on leather hinges.

Over a hundred degrees inside, it was almost impossible to breathe. The cabin was an incubator for tempers ready to explode. Into this oven stepped Otero's group unannounced, though not unexpected. Acting the role of undisputed master of Estancia Springs Ranch, James Whitney sat at the small table ramrod straight and arrogant. His brother-in-law, Alexander Fernandez, lounged on a bunk. Next to him sat Arthur Bailache, Whitney's friend and ranch foreman-in-waiting.

Everyone in the bunkhouse flinched and tensed at the

sound of Martín's rifle shot. Armijo opened the door and glanced out briefly and anxiously. He nodded encouragingly to Otero as he pulled his head back in. Whitney pretended not to care. Besides Otero and Henriquez, Fernandez and Whitney had pistols in their waistbands. Whitney boasted of being a deadly shot, but no one had ever seen him demonstrate his skills. With six angry men crowded into the small cabin, each jockeying for elbow room, little space was left over for movement or rational action.

"I'm Manuel Otero. This is our ranch and bunkhouse. Whitney, if you can show us a writ of possession from the court or a writ dispossessing us, we'll leave. But we both know no judgment has been handed down. So we all know you have neither. By what right do you think you're here?"

Whitney immediately lost his temper.

"I bought the Sandoval Grant which includes Estancia Springs. This is my property, goddamnit."

Just as short-tempered, Otero snapped back, "You're a liar. No court decision and no writ exists."

Hoping to goad Whitney into another intemperate statement, he added, "I thought your brother bought the grant. He was ill-advised."

"None of your goddamned business who bought it, Otero. I've got a writ of possession up at Antelope Springs. If you don't believe me, go up there and get it. No greaser is going to question me about ownership or tell me what to do. Now you and your greaser friends get off my ranch."

All knew Whitney was lying. A bad mistake. Calling the Otero party "greasers" was just as bad. Suggesting they go to Antelope Springs on a fool's errand was an insult.

Otero struggled to check his temper. "We're not moving until you show us, right now, a writ of possession or some other legal right for you to be on this property."

Whitney seemed determined to make mistakes. He pulled the pistol from his waistband and waved it in Otero's face. "Here's my writ. Look at it, you son-of-a-bitch. You've got ten seconds to get out of this cabin and ten minutes to get off my ranch."

Whitney's final error was not checking on his support group, the seven *pistoleros* neutralized by Martín's Winchester. With Whitney's pistol threatening them, Otero and Henriquez pulled theirs, as did Whitney's brother-in-law Fernandez who rose menacingly from the bunk. Only a table width separated the two groups in the hate and heat-filled room. With Fernandez's pistol almost touching his head, Otero fired, killing him instantly with a bullet through the eye socket. His body rolled partially under the bunk. Bailache and Armijo, neither armed, wisely fled the cabin.

Outside, everyone tensed at the sound of gunfire. Martín's Winchester never wavered from Baird's midsection. In the few seconds the gunfight lasted, not one gunman moved to help his employer.

Unnerved, Whitney fired wildly and repeatedly at point-blank rage. One shot tore through Otero's right carotid artery just below his jaw. Mortally wounded, Otero reeled against the door which fell outward, torn off its leather hinges. Down the door frame he slid, every beat of his heart pumping blood from the artery. It spurted between his fingers as he desperately tried to close the jagged tear in his neck.

From close range Whitney volleyed shots with Henriquez. Only once did he score, hitting the doctor in the wrist above his left hand. Coolly, Henriquez shot just twice. His first shattered Whitney's jaw, the second his gun hand.

Straddling the downed figure on the floor, pistol pressed into Whitney's unwounded cheek, Henriquez yelled, "Give up now? Do you surrender?"

Unable to speak, Whitney nodded weakly. Henriquez dragged him out of the airless room, the eyes of both men burning from billows of acrid smoke. In ten seconds six shots had been fired, one at Fernandez, immediately fatal, another, soon to be, at Otero, the rest between Henriquez and Whitney. Henriquez, now all doctor, lifted Otero and laid him on a bunk in the blood-spattered cabin slowly clearing of smoke. His quick look at Fernandez half under another bunk told him the man was dead. Otero still breathed, barely. With no surgical clamps to staunch the flow of arterial blood, the doctor could only stand in sorrow and watch his brother-in-law bleed to death.

Carrying Whitney, Henriquez stepped out under the small front *portal* to lay the badly wounded man on the puncheon floor. The *Tejanos* looked at his inert body without emotion and into the cabin where they could see Fernandez's feet protruding from under a bunk. Their only remaining ally, Whitney's friend Bailache, had rushed out the door as the gunfight began, hardly leadership they wanted to follow.

Now unemployed, the *Tejanos* were hardly out of work. Whitney's cattle still milled around the shallow lake at Estancia Springs. After dark and with care, persuading these cattle to go west would not be too difficult. The seven mounted and rode out of earshot to meet beyond the lake. As before, Baird seemed to be in charge.

Martín, watching carefully, could see Baird gesturing. After a brief discussion, five of the riders feinted an unconvincing move toward the southwest. Baird rode off in the direction of Manzano with his friend Corcoran. Of the seven, only the Mexican, Pecho Torres, looked back. As he left, he turned, seemed to smile, and brushed his hand carelessly across the brim of his *sombrero.* A small salute or an unconscious gesture? Martín wasn't sure.

Under the *portal,* out of the sun, Whitney writhed in agony. Henriquez examined the powder burns on his face from close-range shooting, minor compared to his shattered lower jaw. Whitney's teeth showed through the torn flesh of the cheek. From the skin of his right hand protruded several knuckles and torn cartilage. With what few rags Henriquez could find, he bandaged both wounds. On a mattress from a cabin bunk he and Martín carefully laid Whitney in the back of a ranch wagon. Next to him they placed the body of his brother-in-law, Fernandez. When

Whitney's friend Bailache returned from where he had fled, the doctor told him to drive Whitney to St. Vincent's Hospital in Santa Fe as fast as the wounded man could stand it. Then he bandaged his own damaged wrist, a painful but not serious wound. In another wagon on another mattress they laid Otero's body, torn throat carefully covered with a scarf, his corpse wrapped in a blanket.

News of Otero's killing traveled fast. Mexican and Anglo ranchers, neighbors with whom Otero had shared precious water, forgot their sometimes bitter differences to gather in homage to this generous, popular man. All swore vengeance on Whitney who, fortunately for him, was well on his way to Santa Fe.

Henriquez convinced Whitney's *vaqueros,* standing around in confusion, to keep his cattle at Estancia Springs until the doctor decided what to do with them. He promised they would be paid one way or another.

Jesus Chavez appeared, shattered by Otero's death, but said, *"A sus ordones,"* Dr. Henriquez."

"As before, Jesus, you're in charge of Estancia Springs Ranch. Señor Armijo and I will send further instructions soon as to what to do with the Whitney cattle."

Though forewarned of Whitney's takeover, the sheriff and his posse arrived too late to do anything but calm angry ranchers and try to sort out details about the gunfight. Henriquez and Armijo, the latter embarrassed at having fled the shooting, were questioned closely. Martín, who stayed by the cattle pens out of the way, was not.

Many ranchers joined the escort for Otero's body on its long, slow trip to La Constancia. To bring news of the tragedy to La Constancia before word got there some other way, Carlos Armijo rode out immediately. Ernesto Henriquez and Martín sat their horses at the corral and watched the sad procession until it was out of sight.

CHAPTER 14

NEWS OF THE KILLING was sure to reach Manzano quickly. Martín's family would assume the worst, that he had also been killed or injured. A detour to his home would reassure them.

"Doctor, I'll rejoin you and the cortege later. I must stop at home in Manzano."

Henriquez understood. Almost dragging the spare horse, Pizarra needed no urging once he knew he was on his way to Manzano. Three hours of riding into a declining but still hot sun put them in town just as it was composing itself into shadowless twilight.

Martín approached Manzano from the south so as to talk to Charles Kusz in his office for a minute. Through the window of the kitchen Martín could see a table lamp lighting Kusz's early dinner. Wrapping Pizarra's reins and the lead rope of his second horse around the hitchrail, he called to Kusz as he walked inside. Surprised to see Martín and in such evident distress, Kusz stopped eating.

On the verge of saying something else, he checked himself and said, "What's the matter, amigo?"

"Don Manuel is dead. Killed by Whitney."

Out poured the rest of the bitter story. Kusz shook his head in disbelief.

"My God! How awful for Otero's family. What a loss to the valley and the rest of us! Martín, don't look like that! I know you did everything you were asked, probably more. Whitney got what he deserves. Hope the son-of-a-bitch dies!"

Abruptly Kusz stopped talking, lowered his head, unnecessarily cleared his throat, and ran a hand over his face. Then he looked at Martín out of the corner of his eye. "You haven't heard about Ofelia, have you?" certain he had no chance to.

Martín's head snapped up in alarm. Never had he known Kusz to be reticent.

After another short pause, he sucked in his breath and murmured, "God, why do I have to be the one to tell you?" Then he straightened his back and looked his friend in the eye.

"Two days ago Ofelia was raped by a man named Baird. A friend of his, Corcoran, tried and failed. Both are part of Whitney's *Tejano* posse, I'm pretty sure. Neighbors found her, telegraphed your parents in Albuquerque who came back and are taking care of her. Outside the shock, which must have been God-awful, I'm sure she'll be all right."

The color drained from Martín's face, then it turned red as fury replaced horror.

"And I had a chance to kill that bastard this morning."

The last thing Kusz saw was the pulsing in his friend's temples. A pistol shot pulverized a pane in the kitchen window, and the lamp on the table disappeared in a spray of glass and kerosene. A second bullet, fired a moment later, penetrated Kusz's skull just below the left ear, exiting the other side of his head. Instantly dead, Charles slumped, sightless gaze still on Martín, broken only when his chair tipped over backward. Head on the floor, Kusz lay in the pool of blood seeping from his skull. His legs still hung over the seat of the capsized chair.

Shoulder first, forearm protecting his face, Martín hurled himself through what remained of the kitchen window, taking its wood mullions with him. Several feet beyond its wreckage he hit the ground on his side and immediately rolled into a kneeling position. So instantaneous had been his reaction that the two gunmen were still trying to mount their horses ground-tethered during the shooting. One made it into the saddle and tore south down the main road of town.

The second had trouble mounting. Spooked by the shots, his horse reared and back-pedaled away. Desperately he clung onto the reins while glancing over his shoulder at Martín rushing toward him. Dropping them, the man vaulted into the saddle with the help of its horn. Unable to slip his feet into the stirrups, his seat was precarious. With his left hand Martín grabbed the cheek strap of the horse's bridle and jerked its head sharply toward him. With the right he clutched the rider's gunbelt and yanked him out of the saddle. He felt but never saw the pistol barrel that bloodied the side of his head. Before the gunman could swing again or shoot, he fell heavily to the ground, jarring the pistol from his hand. Martín kicked it away as the man scrambled to his feet. In front of him stood Jack Baird.

From the sheath on the back of his belt Baird pulled a Bowie knife, twelve inches of blade, on its upper side two and a half inches of vicious ripping edge that ran out to the tip.

In a voice strained by his crouching position, he said, "Well, greaser, les see what you can do against this sticker without yore rifle."

In the dying light of the summer evening Martín saw the glint on his opponent's knife blade. He cleared his mind of everything, even hatred of Baird. To the man's surprise, from the unnoticed scabbard on the back of his belt Martín pulled his own razor-sharp knife.

Feet apart, the right foot slightly to the front, Martín stood with body and head well back. With the knife in his right hand, blade tipped slightly up, he put his thumb back of the guard at the base of the grip. As a counterbalance, he held his left hand away from and a little above the waist. Baird took one look at Martín's stance and realized the man he faced was no amateur. For several moments they simply stood there staring at each other. Attracted by the shots, men from the town gathered to watch, staying well out of the way.

Both men were right-handed. Martín wanted Baird to make the first move. He did. Circling to the right, natural for a right-hander, Baird lunged. Martín easily caught the thrust on his blade, letting it run down to the guard before parrying it. Now it was his turn. To confuse Baird he switched the knife to his left hand, faked a lunge which invited the response he hoped for. As Baird stepped forward to thrust, Martín half-stepped nimbly to his right, opposite the direction Baird anticipated. He missed badly, slashing at air, cursing him as he did so. Martín switched his knife back to his right while continuing to circle left, a countermove to further confuse his opponent. He faked another lunge and stepped quickly to the right to avoid the response.

Baird had learned something from Martín's style of fighting, but not enough. He adjusted his return thrust more to his left, narrowly missing Martín's wrist. As Baird's knife arm was fully extended by the thrust, Martín reached across his own body to slash the arm's inner, upper side. Hurt, furious Baird lost his head, handling the knife recklessly, much like a sword. Most thrusts Martín parried, giving ground as Baird pressed his savage attack. Baird scored with a cut on Martín's wrist above his knife hand, laying open the skin to the bone but damaging no tendons. Baird's pupils dilated with the joy of seeing his opponent bleed. Pain had not yet reached his wound, and Martín refused to be distracted by blood flowing down the back of his hand. Though winded by the violence of his attack, Baird was still unpredictable and dangerous.

Time to change tactics again, especially the tempo of the fight. Martín no longer gave ground. Baird, confused, took an apprehensive step backward, as Martín slowly stalked him, bright blue eyes fixed on his. Sweat ran down Baird's face from effort and fear. Martín saw only the latter. Baird's usually slicked-back hair, now wet with perspiration, fell on either side of his skull. He knew something terrible was coming, but not how to stop what he had started.

As if warding off a blow, Martín invitingly extended his left forearm. Unable to resist the bait, Baird lunged, driving his knife to the hilt into the tempting target. With immense effort and gut-wrenching pain, Martín twisted his forearm forward and down, locking the knife into the wound. Baird did not dare let go of his weapon, and it was impossible to withdraw it. With a quick step forward, Martín drove his own blade deep into Baird's stomach, twice. Mouth open from the force of the thrusts, Baird looked up, coughed, and dimly saw Martín's cold blue eyes filled with hate and contempt.

Without a sound, he painfully withdrew Baird's knife from his forearm and threw it on the ground. After wiping his own blade on the dead man's clothes, he awkwardly sheathed it. Cradling the torn arm with his bloody right hand, he stood for a moment, dizzy, loathing himself for what he had just done. Bystanders moved forward to help. To slow the copious flow of blood, one quick thinker wrapped the arm in his kerchief. Martín's right hand was crudely wrapped, too.

As the closest doctor was forty-five miles away in Belen, someone said, "Take him to doña Armendina."

"Doña" was the courtesy title of señora Armendina, the local curandera, viewed as somewhere between healer and *bruja,* a witch.

Too proud to accept a helping hand, Martín stumbled light-headed toward her house. A boy, reluctant to leave the scene of such unexpected excitement, had been sent ahead at a run to tell the *curandera* her help was needed. When Martín staggered into the lamp-lighted room, doña Armendina gently pushed him onto her still-warm, just-vacated bed. A large kitchen table, a chair that in better days sported a back and a makeshift altar completed the inventory of her sparse furnishings. Over the table she threw a threadbare blanket and told the onlookers to move Martín from the bed onto it, then shooed them out.

For more than fifty years doña Armendina had lived in this home, one of Manzano's few structures made entirely of adobe. The small altar was crowded with a Bible, prayer book and dried fronds from the previous spring's Palm Sunday mass. *Nichos* built into the adobe walls held *santos* looking almost alive as their shadows undulated in the moving flames of votive candles in front of each. On crude shelves stood jars of ointments. From vigas hung her *remedios,* dozens of curing plants and herbs, tied in bunches, each picked at the peak of their strength, washed in clear water and hung to dry.

Not a *bruja* but an intensely religious woman, doña Armendina believed her power to heal came from God. Unlike other healers in the area, she was a *curandera total,* using all methods, herbs, massage, ritualism and symbolism, to heal. She was well aware that her success more often depended on the patient's confidence in her and belief in God than on her skills.

Martín's deathly pale face caused her to feel for his pulse, which was strong and regular. She turned toward her crude altar, praying in a voice intended as much for her patient as the Deity.

"*En el nombre de Dios te voy a curar.*" She unwrapped the bloody kerchief to examine his wound by the light of a lamp placed next to his arm.

"What have you done? At least your wound is clean."

Baird's knife was the only unsoiled thing about him.

"You are very fortunate, *hijo*. The blade that made this went all the way through your forearm, but neither of the bones seem harmed."

The cut was wider than the blade that pierced it, and the damage had been increased by Martín's forcing Baird's knife hand downward in the final paroxysm of the fight.

"You should know what I'm going to do," said the curandera.

He was too weak to care.

"First, I will bathe your wound, then use herbs to help stop the bleeding and start the healing."

Fresh spring water washed away blood and cleaned the gaping tear. Carefully she packed into both sides of it yellowish, powdered yarrow, "wound wort," to promote healing. To stop the hemorrhaging, she had mixed with the yarrow ground *yerba mansa,* "lizard tail," a strong herbal hemostat and antiseptic. To help stop the bleeding, on both sides of the wound she plastered sheets of cobwebs. Over everything she wrapped and tied a clean cloth, boiled in water and dried in front of the fire. From two kerchiefs she fashioned a sling. Finally, she dressed the deep cut on the back of Martín's right hand, then washed the dried blood off the side of his face.

Martín sat up, but finding himself dizzy, did not object when doña Armendina gently pushed him back down on the table.

"Descansar usted hijo, para un momento."

The need to see his sister competed with pain and weakness. In minutes he sat up again, head clearing but still somewhat dizzy and disoriented. This time the curandera did not try to stop him and refused the offer of money.

"I think you have done a service for many others who live in this village. *Vaya con Dios."*

Martín thanked her profusely and made a mental note to send her a load of firewood for the winter. After standing a few minutes, the dizziness went away. Someone brought his horses. He accepted a leg up into the saddle, and painfully rode off on Pizarra, trailing the second horse. Unable to unsaddle Pizarra or even open the stable door, Martín rode directly to the *portal* of the house, dropped his reins in exhaustion and slid off the horse. A spasm of pain doubled him over the hitchrail. Steadied by Pizarra's nose in the middle of his back, he recovered enough to cross under the *portal* and enter the *sala.* Inside, his knees started to buckle, so he leaned against the door.

Aaron, coming from the kitchen with fresh water, was

astonished to see his son slumped against the door, pale as death, face swollen, one bandaged hand, and a crude sling supporting the other arm. In just a few days his father seemed to have aged years, become inches shorter. Each stared at the other, came together in the center of the room to bury their faces on each other's shoulder.

Pushing his son away to look at him, Aaron said, "My God, what happened to you?"

Martín looked back with almost lifeless eyes and said in a low monotone, "Otero was killed by Whitney at Estancia Springs. Kusz has been shot and killed in his home a short while ago. There was a fight. I killed Jack Baird, the man who killed Kusz and raped Ofelia."

This was more than Aaron could absorb.

"Daisy," he yelled, "quick, come here."

From Ofelia's room she hurried down the hall, took one look at her son and clapped her hand over her mouth so as not to cry out. Tears streaming, she threw her arms around him.

"Both my babies," Daisy choked out.

When she calmed down, Martín briefly told her what had happened.

She threw her arms around him again and breathed, "You're alive!" Then, "Let's go see her. Ofelia so wants to see you."

The badly blackened eye, bruises and swelling around her broken nose were painfully visible as he approached his sister now sitting up in her bed. He could not bring himself to think about her other hurts. With a self-conscious smile she held her arms out to him, then her face fell as her eyes dropped to Martín's bandages.

He had thought of a dozen ways to tell her about Baird. They fled his mind.

In a choked voice Martín simply said, "He's gone. I killed him."

The sadness on her face fell away, replaced by a look of profound relief. Uncharacteristically, his eyes teared over.

With effort, he got to his feet and turned his head. She tried to ask him a question.

Finger on his lips, he said in a loud whisper, "It was a small price to pay. You know the old 'dicho,' *'Lo que puede'* — what's possible is enough."

Back in the *sala* he questioned his parents in detail about his sister. Except for the shock and shame, she was recovering quickly.

To avoid their hearing inflated accounts later, he told them sketchily about the killing of Otero, which particularly shocked Aaron, the assassination of Kusz, and the fight with Baird. Dazed, Aaron shook his head in disbelief, hating himself for the part he had unwittingly played in the string of tragedies.

Martín stirred restlessly.

"I owe it to don Manuel's wife and daughter to go back to La Constancia for the funeral."

"I know you're tough, Martín, but it's crazy to start now with those wounds. Rest here for a while. That cortege's got a long, slow way to go."

His father steered him out under the front *portal*.

With a look of pain and sorrow he had never seen on his father's face, Aaron said, "Martín, I've been a goddamned fool about so many things. This is a poor time to explain or apologize. But for God's sake forgive me, as best you can."

He knew what that statement had cost his father. Painfully, he reached out and put his hand on Aaron's arm.

"You're not the only one who's made mistakes."

There had been too much of everything. His arm and hand hurt more than he cared to admit. In addition to pain, he was wrung out by successive waves of emotion: Otero, Kusz, the killing of Baird, seeing Ofelia, and now his father's admissions. He stumbled and clutched at the rail under the *portal*.

"I didn't know how tired I was. Lying down sounds good. But I need a favor from you, Father." Nodding in the direction of his horse, "I've ridden poor Pizarra almost into the ground. Could I borrow your chestnut mare for this trip?"

"Hell, yes. Now for heaven's sake, go rest. I'll take care of Pizarra and saddle my mare in a couple of hours. Guess that second horse is from La Constancia. Take my sorrel, too. Trailing two horses'll slow you a bit going, but a spare mount could be helpful coming back.

"If it weren't for Otero's funeral, I wouldn't think of letting you go. You look terrible! Now that's a dumb thing to say," he added smiling, the first Martín had seen.

Daisy unfolded the *colchone* on a *banco* in the *sala,* covered Martín. Instantly he fell asleep. Hours later she reluctantly wakened him. His arm and hand had stiffened painfully. At the hitchrail stood his father's chestnut. Martín's tack, feed for the horses, food and water, even the Winchester in its scabbard, all securely lashed to the saddle. On long lead ropes were Aaron's sorrel and the horse from La Constancia. His father winced with sympathetic pain as he helped his son into the saddle.

Martín looked down at him and said, "I'll take care of both horses, *muchas gracias.*"

CHAPTER 15

EXCEPT FOR THE DIM LIGHT of the moon slipping over the east side of the Manzanos, nothing helped Martín's painful ride south from town, through Punta del Agua, around the end of the mountains, and into Abo Pass. He knew the cortege would take the wagon road there. As expected, the funeral train — wagon and mourners — were camped at Ojo de Abo. Martín arrived quietly, spoke to no one, and spread his blankets outside the edge of firelight.

In the morning he found Ernesto Henriquez and, without mentioning Ofelia, described briefly what happened in Manzano. The doctor was appalled at the assassination of Kusz, a man he found difficult to like, but whose courage and convictions he admired. He took grim satisfaction in the news of Baird's death.

Unable to resist professional curiosity, Ernesto said, "May I look at your wounds?"

Also a bit skeptical about the techniques of *curanderas,* Martín was happy to oblige.

After looking at the tear in his forearm, the doctor said, "Interesting treatment, but the wound's very clean, even showing signs of healing. I have to say she's done a very competent job. Without means of stitching it up, there's not a thing I could have done to improve on it."

When it moved on again, the cortege's slow pace over the almost barren plain to La Constancia was welcome to

Martín, pained by almost any movement. Several miles from the *hacienda* Tranquilo Villareal appeared at a gallop. The reality of seeing the wagon with Otero's covered body was too much for him. Tears rolled uncontrollably down his cheeks. Ernesto and Martín offered what comfort they could. Less than an hour later they were at La Constancia. Men, many crying, *sombreros* in hand, lined the short distance from the front gate to the mesquite doors of the *zaguan*. Their wives, dressed in black or with black *rebosas* over their heads, restrained uncomprehending children clinging to their legs. From Belen, Tome and other nearby towns mourners arrived on horseback, by buckboard or in simple carts to pay their last respects to a man who had been more than just a neighbor and friend.

Past weeping doña Margarita and Catalina, don Manuel's corpse was carefully carried into the *sala* where only days before there had been gaiety and celebration. On a trestle table his body was gently laid, a pillow under his head, votive candles at each corner.

Catalina's face lit up when she saw Martín, a look that turned to distress at the sight of his sling, bandages and pale face. His obvious pain and fatigue prompted her to move to where he was leaning against a wall.

She slipped her hand under his right arm, pressed it softly, and whispered, "Tell me later."

Martín was moved that she should have concern left over for him. With more mourners than anyone anticipated, Manuel Otero's wake started spontaneously. Food was laid out in the *comedor*. Fatigue overcome by hunger, Martín gorged himself. If only temporarily, the food revived him. He returned to the *sala* feeling he should stay with Otero's body. Using the wall for support, he slumped against it and watched as silent women knelt by the body and prayed in sorrow, their husbands behind them, heads bowed, twisting hats in restless hands.

Overcome by fatigue, he could no longer stand or think and made his painful way upstairs to collapse fully dressed on his bed. In minutes Martín was in a restless sleep filled with ragged dreams. Throbbing in the torn muscles of his forearm and from the deep cut above his right hand kept his sleep light. Still exhausted, too pained to sleep, he sat up and soundlessly went down the stairs, then crossed silently into the patio. Its bubbling fountain gave the illusion that the courtyard was cooler than his bedroom. Cradling his bandaged arm, he sat on the edge of the fountain's round basin.

Embarrassed that the pain made him feel sorry for himself, he wondered about the pain of loss felt by Catalina and her mother, the uncertainty of their future and that of the estancia. A movement on the patio startled him. Just as startled was Catalina. In her nightdress under a light robe left heedlessly open, bare feet comfortable on the still warm flagstones, she walked slowly and without embarrassment to within inches of him.

"I couldn't sleep either."

She smiled almost apologetically, then looked at him anxiously.

"Ernesto told us only what he knew about Manzano. There must be more. How badly hurt are your arm and hand?"

Something deeper than affection appeared in Catalina's face. Once, in a rare moment of insight and candor, his father told him that only the young can bear grief and love together. Martín felt this now. He needed to talk to someone who might understand his inner turmoil and doubts. Who better than Catalina? Once started, he couldn't stop. Over the dam of his reticence flowed every hidden thought, feeling of confusion and doubt he ever had. How he had disliked his father, Aaron's misalliance with Whitney, of his friend and mentor Charles Kusz whose advice brought him to La Constancia, his feelings of affection for Otero, of his willfulness that led him to Estancia Springs, and what had happened there.

Last, he gave Catalina an unvarnished version of his

brief visit with Charles Kusz, the shock of hearing of his sister's rape, Kusz's assassination, the fight with Baird, his wounds, and the wrenching visit with Ofelia.

Wise enough to know Martín was a man who probably had never shared intimate thoughts, Catalina sensed the uniqueness of the moment, sat quietly, distracted from her own concerns, and welcomed his trust. In the abundant starlight Martín could see Catalina's large green eyes fixed unblinkingly on his. How surprisingly easy it was to talk to her.

She glanced at his forearm. Blood had begun to seep through the bandages Ernesto had not changed. Without hesitation or self-consciousness, she tore from the front of her nightgown enough cloth to temporarily staunch the bleeding. It was a gesture as revealing of her character as it was of her legs. Despite his pain and the awkwardness of his sling, he pulled her tightly to him. She clung as tightly to his neck. Nothing was awkward about their long, deep kiss. His bandaged right hand fumbled for her breast under the nightgown. Gently, with no resistance from Catalina, he cupped its firm warmth. Holding and kissing each other, they parted reluctantly, breathlessly, and for the first time they laughed. Each realized the absurdity of using an occasion of mourning to demonstrate their love for the other, to experience such passion.

"*Te amo*, Catalina," he said quietly.

"*Te amo tambien*, Martín," she whispered.

The throb in his forearm dizzied him, forcing him to sit again on the edge of the fountain, exhausted by pain and ardor. Catalina watched him anxiously, and when he seemed somewhat recovered, led him to the kitchen and turned up its dim kerosene light. She sat him on the edge of the kitchen table herself on a chair to inspect his wounds at eye level. He had total confidence in her skills. She unbandaged his torn forearm and looked at his wound without flinching. Rubbed raw from riding, it was healing poorly, appeared inflamed, but from the smell of it, not infected. On the wound she left the herbs used by doña Armendina, then rebandaged it with layers of clean cloth. Though the cut above his right hand was healing well, she cleaned and rebandaged it, too.

Bitter tea made from dried wild lettuce leaves is a proven analgesic and sedative. Catalina made him drink two hot cups of it. She watched while he drank, and when he was through, smiled, and they kissed once more. Gently steering him up to his room, Catalina resisted the temptation to enter, but took a goodnight kiss. Quietly closing the door, he fell on his bed, instantly asleep, this time without dreams.

Tranquilo, somber of face and dress, woke him in the morning. He asked after his health and placed a tray of hot chocolate, toast and honey on a table. Martín felt rested, drank and ate everything. Pain lingered in his forearm, but was bearable. Warm sun filtering through gathering clouds and partially closed shutters shone hesitantly. He stretched his sleep away until his forearm hurt him too much. Last night must have been a fantasy. Had he revealed too much of himself to Catalina? Had he actually touched her, kissed her? The reality of don Manuel's funeral brought present sorrow flooding back. His arms fell to his sides. Today would be relieved only by the memory of what he had shared with Catalina.

His vest and *colzones,* appropriately black, were wrinkled and dusty. He doubted if the mourners would notice, but made short work of the dust with a damp towel before putting on his only fresh linen shirt.

Downstairs, the Otero women, Carlos and his wife, and Ernesto Henriquez were waiting for him. They had eaten little breakfast. At the entrance to the *zaguan* Tranquilo, long of face, sat in the driver's seat of a well-worn coach, reins in hand. Martín climbed up to ride with him. The others sat in the body of the coach. Ernesto chose to ride his horse to avoid crowding them.

A formal hearse had been brought from Belen to La Constancia to bear Otero's body. Glass-sided, drawn by black horses, headstalls adorned with black plumes, its strange elegance made the Otero women uncomfortable, so they dismissed it. Instead, they used a simple farm wagon draped in black, a more appropriate conveyance for the unassuming don Manuel's remains. His casket, made on the estancia, was as plain as the wagon that carried it.

The cortege formed slowly. In front, the makeshift hearse, next, the family coach, then mourning friends driving or riding. Finally came many of the workers from the estancia, wives riding burros, husbands walking. Clouds thickened. From over the Manzanos a faint rumbling could be heard. In the Oteros' coach not a word was spoken on the drive to Tome, no one wanting to intrude on the private thoughts of others. As they approached the town's small church, its bell interrupted the silence with the somber *doble,* one short peal followed by two longer ones.

Before the facade of the Church of the Immaculate Conception, the long cortege accordioned to a stop. Ernesto dismounted and helped Carlos and four other pallbearers carry the basket up the steps. Martín walked behind them, followed by the Oteros. Father Ralliere, in a long black cope, stood on the top step of the entrance formally welcoming the body of don Manuel. He nodded gravely to Martín. As the six carried the casket through the deep entrance, a misty rain began to fall. They moved slowly down the dimly lighted nave and set the coffin on a low table in front of the altar. An acolyte removed Ralliere's cope and replaced it with a black chasuble. Solemn music wrung from an ancient hand-pumped organ accompanied the choir standing in galleries flanking the altar.

Family, close friends and workers from La Constancia filled every pew. Those just curious stood in back of the church or outside front doors left open because of the moist, stifling hear. Limited ventilation was taxed by the combined odors of flowers, candle smoke, incense and unbathed mourners.

The ringing of the *doble* ceased, along with the choir and plaintive organ music. After a moment's silence punctuated by the congregation coughing and shifting to a more comfortable position on hard pews, an assistant priest read the scriptures. Father Ralliere then mounted the pulpit to deliver the homily, an eloquent review of what most already knew about the deceased; don Manuel Otero, good husband and father; a generous, helping friend to his neighbors. His care of the people who worked at La Constancia exceeded by a wide margin anything expected of an employer. For the benefit of others who also had workers, Ralliere obliquely suggested that this might have been one of the reasons for Otero's success. Despite wealth, he remained a simple, courteous, courageous man. The homily was followed by mass and communion.

Trailed by family and mourners, Otero's casket was slowly carried out to the wet *campo santo,* the small cemetery immediately adjacent to the church. At graveside Father Ralliere blessed don Manuel's last resting place, and after prayers, committed his soul to God. As the casket was lowered into the ground, doña Margarita turned away, crying bitterly, and had to be supported by Catalina and Carlos. Surreptitiously wiping his eyes, Martín followed the family back to the coach.

In a patch of damp, unkempt grass next to the church lay an unmounted bronze bell. As she passed it, Catalina gently disengaged herself from her mother, stopped and waited for Martín.

With the faintest trace of a smile she said, "Do you remember when my father told you his father and Ralliere were bitterly at odds over water? Afterwards, my grandfather fell very ill and persuaded a reluctant Ralliere to pray for his recovery. When Grandfather finally did recover, he and Grandmother gave that bell to the church.

"But Father Ralliere got in the last word. He had both their names chiseled off the bell which has never been hung or rung."

CHAPTER 16

TO HIS WIFE AND DAUGHTER Manuel Otero's loss was devastating, emotionally and practically. By working themselves to the point of exhaustion each day, they almost avoided thinking about him. But in the evening, particularly doña Margarita would often lower her head and weep silently, handkerchief crushed in her fist.

It was easy for Martín for persuade himself to stay at La Constancia for a while. Margarita relied more and more on his judgment and decisions relating to the estancia. With no objection from the mother or daughter, his stay stretched into several weeks. Catalina tended his health like a mother hen, and his wounds improved daily. In a letter to his family he explained most of the reasons for his delay.

As he did at home, and with Margarita's willing agreement, he carefully reviewed the estancia's accounts, collecting debts which the generous Manuel had allowed to fall overdue, and brought the books up to date. Then the September harvest needed organizing. With Tranquilo's help, Martín worked out schedules, choice of field bosses, arrangements for storage or transportation of the crops. Once the harvest was underway, he knew it was time to leave. He also knew that he and Catalina loved and needed each other, that it was only a question of time until his return.

"*Es la hora,* Catalina. I've got to go mend my relationship with Father. I need to see Ofelia, too."

She understood. He worried about leaving Margarita and Catalina to manage alone. Even with Tranquilo's help and that promised by the always-busy Carlos, how could these inexperienced women manage the estancia? What about the still unresolved Whitney claim to a portion of the Baca Grant?

He and Catalina knew marriage would make them complete. Though her mother had more than an inkling of the depth of their feelings, nothing had been said to her. Traditional form required that a proposal come through Martín's father. If Margarita agreed to the match, he knew marriage would mean a commitment to her, too. Catalina would insist on it. Not only did he have to earn a living, but start doing something on a permanent basis. Her mother had mentioned nothing about a role for him at La Constancia, nor was he sure he would be able to handle it if offered. Tearful goodbyes from the Oteros marked his departure. In pleas for him to return soon, their unspoken need for him tore at his heart. Martín felt no need to hurry back to Manzano. Now astride tireless Pizarra, he didn't know how much "bottom" his father's mare had for the long ride. The led chestnut, also his father's, responded erratically, alternately walking slowly or trotting to catch up. But the leisure of the ride gave him plenty of time to think about his future.

A late start from La Constancia meant another night at Abo Spring. As early dawn was barely outlining the Manzanos, he woke and on a small fire warmed his sparse breakfast. Hot coffee and stale *tortillas* were barely enough and made him yearn for his mother's good cooking only hours ahead. Can Catalina cook, he wondered? Probably yes. She did everything else well.

Early morning sun was a hand's breadth above the horizon when he passed through the dusty village of Punta del Agua and turned north onto the Manzano road. At its junction with the dirt track west into Quarai Mission, suspicion as well as curiosity overcame caution. What possibly could be of enough value there to cause someone to shoot at him? Hesitantly, feeling foolish, he rode just far enough down the dirt track to see the mission's bulk, the remnants of its sandstone flanks a burning rose in early morning light.

As startling as it had been the first time, Martín hardly expected to see another flashing blue light. Again it came from a viga slot near the top of the high wall of the roofless church. But there it was. Twice it blinked. Whoever flashed it couldn't know he was there. With a quick look over his shoulder he saw what he'd missed weeks before, an answering flash from just south of Punta del Agua. Then he was spotted.

A rifle shot caused his mare to buck wildly, jerking hard the lead rope of the led sorrel. Corkscrewed in his saddle from looking at the answering signal, Martín could barely control the mare and was almost thrown. He pulled back on the reins to settle her down. Shot through, the left rein parted just behind the bit. Exposed and vulnerable, he quickly pivoted again in his saddle to spot the rifleman. A second bullet went through the rim of his saddle cantle, just missing his leg. Another shot left a long, bloody gash across his mare's croup.

He needed cover, badly. Without urging, the frantic mare loped up the low hill behind the solid curved wall of the rear of the nave. A quick look at his mount's wound and where he had been, the road below told him the shot came from within the broken walls of the convento. Now behind the nave, he was protected.

Like the thicker mission walls, those of the convento had been built up of flat pieces of local sandstone cemented with adobe mud. Their remnants, about three feet high and a foot thick, offered plenty of protection and concealment for a gunman.

Behind the nave he had the only cover the hill afforded. But protected by the broken walls or inside the church, a gunman was also safe from him. At the moment, having no one to shoot at seemed less important than getting himself and the horses out of the mission area. Up and over the hill was the only way.

Dismounting, staying directly behind the nave, he led both horses over its crest. Not a shot was fired. Once on its reverse slope, he again checked the mare's wound and began to get mad. The bullet was obviously meant for him. It made sense that whatever was going on had to be related to Whitney's takeover of Estancia Springs. Getting even instead of getting out began to appeal to his aggressive nature. He needed little excuse for action. With his still-stiff left forearm, out of its saddle scabbard he awkwardly withdrew the Winchester. With his right hand he fumbled in the saddlebag for a box of cartridges. Unsaddling the mare and freeing the sorrel from the lead rope, he sent both bolting over the hill with sharp slaps on their rumps.

Still protected by the wall of the nave, he walked back up to the top of the ridgeline from where he could see almost all of Quarai and east to minuscule Punta del Agua. From his position he could see far up the gentle cleft of Cañon Sapato west of Quarai ruins. To his surprise, up the canyon cattle, hundreds of them, milled about or grazed, concealed except from where he lay.

How could he have been so stupid not to have guessed the first time he was here? Especially as he had been followed all the way to Manzano. Whitney never knew how his *Tejanos* spent their spare time — rustling. Or maybe he did but didn't care.

Kusz probably knew more than he was telling, or he wouldn't have asked, "What are they doing now?"

That must have been why he was killed.

Two men, bent double, scuttled out of the church into the low-walled ruins of the convento. All he could do was watch them. Odds were at least three to one against him. Another was now bringing up cattle from near Punta del Agua in answer to the blue signal. That made it even worse. Getting even was one thing, but these odds were inviting disaster! Two shots fired simultaneously stung his face with dirt and stone chips. He slid over to better cover. Considering the number of gunmen against him, holding the high ground was cold comfort. Now was the time to get out, to come back with help. Unable to move their rustled stock quickly, especially in daytime, the *Tejanos* would likely still be here when he got back. Straight north over the hill would get him out of this fix. Crouched, ready to run, he took a last look around.

Fifty feet to the east, on top of the ridgeline, he saw a familiar, battered hat and the unmoving body of a man, face down.

"*Por Dios!* It's my father!"

In a bent-over sprint he reached and dragged the limp form over the crest of the hill to lay him gently behind some rocks. As far as he could tell, the bullet wound in Aaron's thigh, and an equally bloody one through his upper arm had broken no bones. But he was in shock, barely conscious. Using both of their neckerchiefs, Martín bandaged the wounds as best he could.

"Bastards stole my cattle," suddenly mumbled Aaron, unaware who was tending him. "Followed the sons-a-bitches down here. They're dangerous."

"I already know that," answered Martín out of breath and with unintended sarcasm. "Stay quiet. I'm your son Martín. I'll get you out. But I'm going to take another look before we go. Almost got shot coming up here. Don't want to get it leaving."

Inching back to the crest of the hill, he was startled to see a man run west from the front of the church and scramble up a nearby slope of broken adobe bricks and pieces of quarried sandstone, the ruins of the large Indian pueblo that Quarai had been built to serve. Apparently the man had been hiding in the nave.

Afraid of being flanked, Martín swung his rifle over to cover the man in the ruins. At the top of the slope of rubble the man dropped prone and fired back toward the mission. He turned, shrugged his shoulders and lightly touched the brim of his *sombrero*. It was Pecho Torres, the Mexican gunman Martín had last seen at Estancia Springs. A total surprise, but at this point he would take help from anyone or anything. One more for us, one less for them.

Medical help for his father was the priority. However, he couldn't just ignore the one rider driving rustled stock toward the mission. The rifle shots would have warned him. Maybe they would swing around behind and cut off his escape route. His father wounded, unconscious, another *Tejano* on his way. He felt trapped. Even with the surprise addition of Torres' help they would be badly outgunned. Leave now, or take chance at improving the odds by wounding or killing a rider? Why not? That man was a rustler and rustling a hanging offense.

Bluffing seven men into inaction at the Springs had been like a card game. Killing the man who shot his best friend and raped his sister sat more easily on his conscience than this. A volley from behind the low walls impacted dangerously close and made up his mind for him. The shots were intended to distract him to allow the rider to labor up the marshy draw toward Quarai and safety. Heading his mount toward the firm footing of the dirt track to the church, he was either ignoring Martín or didn't know he was above him. The rustled cattle, now strung out almost to Punta del Agua, were left to fend for themselves.

At the sight of the rider hell-bent for Quarai, any conscience Martín had about him was drowned by the adrenaline pumping into his veins. One long shot would help the odds. Almost by itself, his rifle swung in his direction. Martín carefully followed the man in his open sights. Now on the hard dirt track his target was moving at a run.

He calculated the lead needed and how far a .44 caliber bullet would drop in two hundred yards, how much to compensate in elevation for shooting downhill. Compressing his whole hand slowly so as not to jerk the trigger, he fired. The slug hit the rider in the right side of his chest. Increased by the horse's forward speed, its impact drove the man back over the cantle of his saddle and down the croup of his mount. Motionless in the dirt, his arms were raised above his head as if in surrender.

Martín dropped his head on the rifle stock. Even at two hundred yards, the killing was too easy, too impersonal. Then reason replaced revulsion. His father was badly wounded. He had improved the odds of their survival, still held the high ground and, hopefully, had a new ally. It fell quiet. He waited.

Although with more men and better cover, the *Tejanos* knew they had a problem on their hands. They now looked, reluctantly, to Rafe Corcoran who had taken Jack Baird's place as leader. At a signal from Corcoran inside the church, the two scrambled from behind the broken convento walls and dashed into its protection. Rafe leaned against an interior wall, breathing hard and tried to encourage his edgy men.

"Look, we got two more'n they. No tellin' what that goddamned greaser Torres'll do. Might stay out there, might come back in. He's got as much at stake as we got, and'll swing for rustlin' same as us if he gets caught.

"We kilt the guy on the hill. The other one is probably jes a greaser, too. Bound to lose his nerve or make a mistake. An' we ain't seen the sheriff in the weeks we been bringin' cattle here."

Spirits buoyed by Corcoran's shaky logic, two of them ran back out to the broken ruins of the convento, reassured that they would be safe behind a thicker portion of it. He kept the other man inside the church to shoot down from its walls.

Checking on his father, Martín found Aaron rolled onto his back, face up in the sun. He pulled him into the scanty shade of a chamisa bush, then returned to his original position. The several rounds he fired into the convento walls ricocheted off, and several shots were fired at him in return. And Torres wasn't able to shoot into the church entrance. Was this a stalemate, wondered Martín? For several minutes nothing happened except quiet.

Shattering the silence was the report of a large calibre rifle. He almost felt the muzzle blast and watched in awe as a rock and mud corner of the convento wall disintegrated. His blood raced.

In excitement he said out loud, "That's got to be Justino Abeyta and his big .50 Sharps buffalo rifle!"

No one else in the valley owned an antique like that. Today, no one would buy such a piece. Sure enough, up the hill north of the mission trudged the stocky figure of Abeyta, the skilled farrier of Punta del Agua, Sharps in hand, all business. He walked casually as if going to a buffalo stand. Not a shot was fired at him.

An awesome weapon at least thirty years old, Abeyta's Sharps was designed for buffalo hunters, and like the buffalo, its time had passed. But today the three-and-a-quarter-inch-long shell filled with one hundred and seventy grains of powder propelling a seven-hundred-grain bullet was a godsend.

Martín had not seen Abeyta since he shoed Pizarra in Punta del Agua many weeks before. With a casual wave he moved up the hill to take advantage of what slight cover the ruins of the old Lucero house offered. Once there, he squatted on his heels and rocked with the recoil of the rifle as he blew another hole in the convento wall large enough to slide an arm through.

Why Abeyta was there wasn't important. The improving odds were, now three against four, two of those four bottled up inside low convento walls now unsafe against Justino's powerful rifle. Martín hoped he had brought plenty of shells.

As both sides of the church and the convento could be covered by Abeyta and Torres, a third man was needed in front to fire into its entrance. He was the only candidate. Getting there was the problem. Martín mimed to Abeyta to stay put, then cautiously worked his way west along the ridge and down to where Pecho Torres lay on the mound of adobe rubble.

Reaching Torres, he said, "I'm Martín Wolf."

"I know," Pecho replied. "My name is Pedro Tonala," knowing Martín didn't believe him. "I happen to like greasers, being one myself. And I sure don't think much of those gringos," thumbing in the general direction of the mission. "Treat me like shit. Nothing but insults. I'm probably even better than them at what we all do.

"A great mistake for me to join that gringo Whitney. For reasons you don't need to know I'm not very welcome in Texas. And for reasons you do know, I don't think I'll be very welcome here. I'll help you with pleasure. Don't think me impolite if you don't see me after this is over.

"Who's the hombre with the cannon on the other side of the mission? Glad he's on our side."

"The big noise is Justino Abeyta, a friend of mine. Don't shoot him."

At this point all Martín could do was trust. He looked at the Mexican.

"*Claro.* Thank you, Pedro. Don't change your mind. My father is up on that hill wounded and unconscious. That's my problem. How about a few rounds into those low walls? Might distract your former friends while I cross that marshy bit south of the entrance. From there I can put a few rounds into the church."

The last thing the *Tejanos* would expect was his making the slow crossing of the soggy ground in front of the mission. Risk would be minimized by surprise and a much improved firing position. Abeyta's Sharps erupted reassuringly just as he began his slogging run. Simultaneously, Torres fired at an angle at the mouth of the half-ruined church and into the convento walls. Once across the swampy ground, Martín dropped for cover behind a fallen cottonwood. To make certain the mission defenders knew they were surrounded on three sides, he pumped two shots into the church.

At another blast into the convento from Justino, a man's head bobbed sickeningly as it appeared momentarily above a wall. Hit either by the bullet or heavy shards of stone, it disappeared quickly. The odds were about even. Martín's confidence grew.

Confidence also made him careless. He slid forward under the cottonwood trunk to get a better shooting angle. Unseen, Rafe Corcoran had climbed high up the interior wall of the church's face to the edge of the deep scallop that once framed a circular window in the front wall. Relatively well protected, Corcoran could now shoot downward.

They must know they're done for, thought Martín. One shell away from his last, he hoped they were. At that moment Corcoran took careful aim at the prone figure. Almost simultaneous with the crack of Corcoran's rifle, Martín's spine, along with his head and both legs, bowed up into an improbable arc. Excruciating pain shot through the base of his vertebrae. Air exploded from his lungs. Stunned by the blow, in pain, gasping for air, he forced himself to look up as he heard Torres, who had moved to a better position, fire a return shot. Corcoran's body pivoted slowly around the edge of the wall and, as it gathered momentum, followed his rifle to the ground.

Certain he had been crippled for life or mortally wounded, Martín felt as if the lower part of his body was on fire. In excruciating pain he twisted around to look. In the sheath shredded by Corcoran's slug was the contorted blade of his "Arkansas Toothpick." By his leg lay its severed haft.

"*Dios.* Twice you've saved me," he murmured and dropped his forehead to the ground.

The feeling of relief did little for the pain in his spine. When he could breathe again, he called out, more of a croak than a shout, but loud enough to let the two *Tejano* survivors know he was still alive and more or less in charge.

"You're surrounded on three sides. As good as dead unless you give up now."

From the mission or convento not a sound. Part of one of its low sandstone ramparts simply disintegrated from another shot by Abeyta. That clinched it. Thrust out of the church entrance on the end of a rifle barrel, a sweat-stained hat signaled the fight was over. At least two, probably more of the gunmen were dead. The "greasers" had won.

In an effort to make himself sound commanding, Martín

loudly croaked, "Everybody out. Hands in the air. No rifles, no pistols, no tricks or you're dead."

"*Hola, compadre.* Guess you're all right," yelled Torres, cautiously rising from the pile of rubble.

"Alive," Martín gasped, "thanks to you."

To be ready for anything, he ejected the empty from his Winchester and watched his last live round rise in the receiver. With the help of his rifle's barrel he pushed painfully to his feet and propped himself against a limb of the fallen cottonwood to shake off the dizziness and breathe normally. Unsteadily, a weak smile on his face, Martín hobbled across the marshy stream toward his Mexican ally. Torres glanced at him, said nothing more, and walked to where the *Tejanos* had tethered their horses. In minutes he chose, saddled and mounted the strongest, then rode up Cañon Sapato at a fast trot. Just before disappearing, he turned and gave Martín a smile and small salute.

"*Mille gracias, amigo,*" Martín managed to call out and saluted back.

First to surrender was the man in the church. He emerged, waited for Martín, his hat still quivering on the muzzle of the rifle. From behind the sandstone walls of the convento came the second, covered with the blood of a third badly wounded, whom he half-carried. Corcoran's body was left where it had fallen. Without being asked, the survivor from the church went down the road for the body of the man shot out of his saddle by Martín at the beginning of the fight.

All of Martín's remaining strength was needed to climb the low hill where he had left his father. Justino kept an eye on the two remaining gunmen.

Semi-conscious, in pain and furious, Aaron stirred. "Son-of-a-bitch, missed the fight."

"You're lucky," murmured Martín.

"Last night heard hooves in our lane. My cattle and their horses. Should've known then. Could even see 'em moving!"

Out of breath, he fell quiet.

"Tell me later," said Martín, watching his father begin to lose consciousness again from the effort of talking.

Reviving again, Aaron talked almost compulsively, still unsure of his audience.

"I was too damn slow. When I got through fumbling the saddle onto my horse in the dark, I could only follow those bastards by sound. They went right down the main street of town, too!"

Martín again tried to stop him. Exhausted, Aaron dropped his head to the ground, then revived once more and felt he had to tell all.

"Spent the night on the back of this hill. First light, came up to look around. Didn't think anybody would be watching. Stupid! Paid for it, too."

Finally recognizing his son, Aaron said, "Martín, they must have hit everybody around here who had any cattle. Hope most of 'em belonged to Whitney."

Up the hill trudged Justino Abeyta, occasionally prodding the two unwounded gunmen ahead of him with his rifle. Their faces were blank. Aaron, pale and weak, looked at Justino with glazed eyes.

"Glad you could join us," he said unsteadily, specially since I couldn't. What the hell you doing here? You don't own any cattle."

"True, señor Aaron. But I cannot afford to lose good customers either. Not that I knew it was you and Martín at first, but I been watching these hombres for weeks now."

"If you suspected them, why didn't you tell somebody?" said Martín.

"I should have. These *Tejanos* thought because almost nobody but me lives in Punta del Agua now, by moving cattle up the canyon below town they wouldn't be seen. When I heard shooting near Quarai, I figured someone might need help. Besides all that, I haven't shot this old *carabina* for years. Wanted to see if it still worked."

He looked at the two sullen gunmen.

"Apparently it does."

One distressed look at Justino told him Martín had to get his father to medical help in Manzano quickly.

"Give me a half-hour. I'll be back with something on wheels."

On an extra horse he tied the limp figure of the wounded man. As their hands were bound, he had to help the other two gunmen into the saddle. On their way to Punta del Agua he followed the three with the rifle balanced on his pommel. In a windowless sandstone warehouse on the edge of town, he securely locked in the three survivors.

Not knowing where the Valencia County sheriff and deputies were, or even if they might show up, Martín left the bodies and weapons where they were. The law could sort out what happened. Unexpectedly the sheriff and his posse appeared, on their way back to Belen from Estancia Springs and drawn by the distant sound of the last shots of the gunfight.

Acutely uncomfortable, Martín lay on the ground hoping to ease the pain in his back. The sheriff walked over and looked down on him with surprise.

"Ain't you Martín Wolf? Didn't expect to see you again. Ya' hurt? Thought you had enough trouble out at the Springs."

Embarrassed at being caught lying down, he answered with a forced smile.

"Did something to my back. I'll be all right directly."

The sheriff looked at him somewhat skeptically. "I'm John Bartlett, sheriff of Valencia County. Heard what you did out at Otero's, but you'd gone before we had a chance to talk."

He eyed the bodies and piled weapons.

With one eye closed he asked Martín, "What the hell's been going on here? Looks like *el termino* for most of Whitney's ex-employees."

Bartlett kept talking, apologizing for being too late getting to Estancia Springs, explaining why they had been delayed.

"Must'a talked to about everybody there but you. Never

heard so many different versions of the same story from so many people. The only ones who were in the cabin when the shooting started, Henriquez, Armijo and Fernandez, couldn't agree who fired the first shot. Henriquez and Armijo said Whitney did. Fernandez, of course, said Otero started it."

Sitting down on a rock, Bartlett removed his sweat-stained hat, wiped the liner, scratched his head.

"Gotta say I never met so many people who agreed on one thing. Most of 'em hated Whitney like he was a rabid coyote. I know I'm supposed to be impartial, but between you and me, I think it was just a matter of time before Whitney got nailed by somebody, even surrounded by those hard cases he hired."

Looking at the bodies stiffening in the sun, Bartlett added, "They don't look so damn hard now, do they? Those hombres drifted pretty quickly outta Estancia Springs 'fore I got a chance to talk to them. I guess it don't make no difference now."

Martín offered, "Whitney apparently didn't know they were rustling on the side. Guess he underpaid them. How'd they get away with so many of his cattle?"

"Well, that's a little embarrassing. Those *Tejanos* came back that night and just took 'em while we were eating supper at a neighboring ranch."

Martín was beginning to like Bartlett. Behind the homespun manner and candor was a lot of shrewdness.

Pointing toward Cañon Sapato, he said, "You can get everybody's cattle back now, sheriff. They're up that draw."

"Well, I'll be damned! That's going to solve a problem for a lot of people in the valley. But there's another you might be interested in, Martín. We heard from Santa Fe that Whitney was lowered out a window at St. Vincent's Hospital and escaped. Probably helped by his brother. Warrants are out for both of 'em."

Bartlett then asked what had happened at the mission. Reluctant to say much, Martín gestured at the bodies.

"This is half of what's left of Whitney's bodyguard. The

live half is already locked up in Punta del Agua. Justino Abeyta's the man who really saved the day here, saved me and my father, too. He's one of the few people who live in Punta."

"Martín, hear you killed a man named Baird up in Manzano. Sort of the *Tejano's* leader. Clear case of self-defense, everybody says. You're in one scrap after another. How the hell did you get involved here?"

"Coming back from Otero's funeral I turned in to see Quarai. I have kind of a 'thing' about this place. First, someone shot at me, nicking my horse. Then I discovered my father lying up on that hill, wounded. Turns out his cattle had been rustled, too, so he followed these gringos down here last night. You've seen the rest of it."

"Don' know how, but I'd say you done right well."

Just then Abeyta creaked up in a springless two-wheeled cart and a look of apology. The ride would be as uncomfortable as traveling in a solid wheel *carreta,* but Martín knew it was the only way they would get to Manzano.

"Justino Abeyta, meet Sheriff John Bartlett."

He embarrassed Abeyta describing his help in the fight. No mention was made of Pecho Torres. Still wondering how so few had accomplished so much, Bartlett decided that the wounded Aaron and stolen cattle up the draw were convincing enough reasons for the fight. He didn't press for more details.

The bodies were searched for some sort of identification, then buried by the sweating deputies in a shallow common grave behind the church. Complaints about the hot work increased when told they had to take three prisoners, one unable to ride, all the way back to Belen.

* * * * *

Barely able to move because of his stiffening spine, Martín began to wonder how he, let alone his father, could make the five miles to Manzano. To cushion the ride, Justino brought a sack of grain. Martín suggested adding saddles and blankets. With Abeyta's help he painfully edged his way into the cart, sat on the sack and leaned against the saddle. He winced in sympathy as Justino gingerly slid in his father's limp body. He lay on the saddle blankets, and Martín steadied his head in his lap. Abeyta caught Aaron's and the two horses led by Martín and tied them all to the cart with lead ropes. Carefully he started the cart on what he knew would be a painful journey to Manzano.

Semi-conscious, Aaron seemed mostly concerned with his conscience and insisted on unburdening himself.

With a glazed look at his son, he said in a hoarse whisper, "Martín, already told you I've been a goddamned fool. Now I've got to tell you I'm a greedy one, too."

"Tell me later, Father."

"No, now. Whitney promised me five thousand acres of his grant if I'd help smooth his takeover of valley ranches on the Baca Grant. What an arrogant, pretentious man!"

"Doesn't make any difference now. Save your strength."

Aaron droned hoarsely on. "Saw refusal in your eyes the moment Whitney asked you to work for him. I was greedy enough to want the land, too stupid to think of the consequences for the family. God! Wish I could take it all back. Especially Ofelia."

Aaron began to cry.

"Guess you think I've been pretty selfish wanting to hang on to you all these years."

That was news. Martín was under the impression his father could care less what he did as long as he did it somewhere else. Aaron's rambling talk cost his pride as much as it pained his body.

Martín did his best to cushion himself and his father from the lurching of the cart. Fortunately, Aaron fainted again. Despite Justino's best efforts to avoid ruts and rocks, five endless miles to Manzano were exquisite torture. They arrived exhausted with pain. Once there, Justino headed straight for the *curandera*.

Surprised to see Martín again, doña Armendina quickly inspected his forearm and nodded approval of its progress.

With effort Justino lay Aaron's unconscious and limp form on the kitchen table. Clucking, the *curandera* probed and cleaned his wounds of debris. She used the same combination of yarrow, yerba mansa and cobwebs, bandaged them all with cloth boiled clean. Despite his loss of blood, she didn't think his wounds were serious.

For Martín's back there was little she could do besides applying a hot poultice and recommend his soaking in hot water as often as possible. Then she raised his chin to better look in his eyes.

"God is watching over you, *hijo*."

The distance to the Wolfs' *hacienda* was mercifully short. Daisy, watering flowers bordering the edge of the *portal*, was trying hard not to think what might have happened to Aaron after he leaped out of bed, cursing, in the middle of the night. At the sound of the cart she turned, saw his limp body and clapped her hands to her mouth. Then she screamed for Ofelia.

Martín watched his sister closely as she ran out of the *sala* toward her father. Bruise shadows showed on her face, her nose was still swollen, but she walked with the light step and vitality that was so much of her personality.

Assured by Justino that Aaron's wounds were hardly mortal, the women helped carry him into the house and lay him on the bed. He regained consciousness long enough to smile weakly at Daisy, then fell into a deep sleep.

Steadied by the indispensable Justin, Martín limped into the *sala* and stretched out on a *banco* layered with blankets. Each painting the other as hero of the affair and omitting many details, they described to Daisy and Ofelia what happened at Quarai. Respecting the Wolfs' privacy, Abeyta refused an invitation to supper and left, but not before Daisy filled a sack with the best of everything she could find in the kitchen.

The men's first days were spent in sleep and rest, and Martín watched in wonder as the new relationship with his father unfolded. It had begun on that torturous ride from

Quarai. Aaron's admission of his mistakes in the Whitney business made a deep impression. Never had he felt so close to him.

Martín had always thought of his father as intelligent, with special talents, certainly hard-working, but Martín had never thought him as prone to making errors in judgment. Reinforced by the loyal Daisy, he and everybody else believed in his infallibility. How startling that Aaron at last admitted to imperfection! He liked the idea of his father with flaws. Now he could judge him as he did any man.

Something else important; his father had stopped drinking.

Until Aaron was wounded, he had clung to his view of Martín as young, impulsive, lurching from one job or design to another. Too busy with his own schemes to notice until convalescence forced him to, Aaron realized his son had grown into a competent, reliable man, capable of leadership, ready to marry, depended on by others. How could he have ignored the seasons of his son's maturing into such an able, likeable man?

Martín also concentrated on improving his relationship with his father. But he had other concerns: his love for Catalina and mental hand-wringing over the two men he had killed.

Raised to value human life, in contrast his contemporaries seemed to value it lightly, perhaps hardened by children dying of unchecked disease, fatalities at logging camps, mines, ranches and deaths from violence in town. Most Mexicans Martín knew had no fear of death. They looked on it as an organic part of life. Like a clay vessel, at some point life is meant to be broken.

Did being half-Mexican make him less sensitive to another's death? Because he lived where people winked at law-breaking was hardly an excuse for killing. Yet he had twice been in situations where immediate action, even killing, seemed more expedient than reasoning. Yet in both instances he could have avoided the killing. No longer did he have Kusz to help him grope toward answers. Now he would look to Catalina, mature in so many unexpected ways, to help him sort through his confusion.

Still limping, Aaron's increasing energy made him restless, while his son's back improved daily. Often they sat together under the front *portal* to soak up the late afternoon sun and talk about the future. One day Martín said what Aaron had been expecting but had not really wanted to hear.

"Father, I know I've talked about Catalina until you're sick of hearing it. This is not a quick affair like others we both know about."

He ducked his head in embarrassment and said, "I want to get married."

Aaron turned and said, "That serious, huh? Martín, this comes as a surprise! I thought maybe you were still sick."

Martín smiled at his father's wry teasing and plowed on.

"I'm certain she wants to marry me. I'm positive her mother and her Uncle Carlos will be favorable, too. Would you write them a letter on my behalf asking for Catalina's hand?"

There went his half-formed plan to turn the *sitio* over to his son, an idea so unformed he had never mentioned it to Martín. How many other opportunities had been missed because of this Whitney affair? But he didn't hesitate with his answer.

"Of course I will. It may sound strange coming from me, but I'm sure you'll get immense satisfaction from your marriage, probably great success in your work. Of the two, my guess is satisfaction's more important.

A week crawled by after Aaron had written the letter of marriage proposal. Impatient for a reply, each evening Martín would recite the litany of Catalina's saintly virtues.

Always there followed the question, "Do you think I could run La Constancia?"

Bored by the repetition, Ofelia said kindly, "Martín, both you and I know those women need you. Besides, to whom else could they turn? So you're not don Manuel. But you've all the skills necessary to keep La Constancia, and probably Estancia Springs, functioning. Stop worrying about the future. Take one step at a time."

Daisy added, "If Catalina is as smart as you say she is, she can't wait for you to come help them out."

Time passed in slow motion. In little more than a week a reply addressed to Aaron came from doña Margarita. After reading it, he handed it and several unopened enclosures without comment to his impatient son.

"*Estimado* sr. Wolf," it read. "My brother, sr. Carlos Armijo, and I believe your son, Martín Wolf, to be a young man of learning, energy and courage. We would be honored and pleased to have him join our family by marriage to my daughter Catalina.

"As soon as an appropriate wedding date can be arranged, we will welcome you, sra. Wolf, and your daughter Ofelia as our guests. *Respectamente,* Margarita Otero."

The first enclosure was from Carlos. "Martín, I join in my sister's welcome to you as a future member of our family. You should know that all is not well at La Constancia. External pressures, mainly from Santa Fe, cast a shadow on its future. I have done what I can, but have many other business affairs to attend to. Your presence will be particularly welcome. It is wanted and needed. *Respectamente,* Carlos Armijo."

Martín read it to his father. A second enclosure, from Catalina, he kept to himself. He blushed as he read it. It was brief.

"Please hurry, *mi caro*. I need you so. C."

"So you start out with a problem," said Aaron. "No marriage I know of is without them. Though this one is earlier and maybe more difficult than you think. I hope not. Move slowly. Don't decide anything too quickly. I know now," he looked away with embarrassment, "that speed and greed don't travel well together."

At dawn the next day Martín set out for La Constancia with his father's bay pulling a light buckboard trailing

Pizarra. The buckboard meant taking the long road around the southern lobe of the Manzanos through Abo Pass, a two-day trip to the Rio Grande.

His few possessions, saddle and blanket, bridle, rifle in its scabbard, extra shells, shaving gear, and all of the few clothes he owned were dumped in the bed of the buckboard. For the horses he packed nosebags and oats, and for himself food cooked and carefully wrapped by Ofelia.

Next morning he needed all his persuasion and strength to get the big gray between the shafts of the wagon. Once accustomed to pulling the rig, Pizarra's long-legged pace ate up the remaining miles to the *hacienda* on the river.

He wished Carlos had been more specific as to what problems lay ahead. Nothing could have prepared Martín for the realities he was about to face.

CHAPTER 18

IN SANTA FE Tom Catron stalked into his office, with his malacca cane slapped the desk like a shot and bellowed, "Find Camp Brown. Now!"

Like a disturbed nest of ants, the clerks scurried about accomplishing nothing. One was level-headed enough to run to Brown's boarding house. Within an hour he appeared with Brown in tow.

"There you are, Brown. About time. I've got a job for you. Now, sit down, goddammit, 'til I get through signing these papers."

Lawyer and autocrat, Thomas B. Catron considered himself, with some justification, the undisputed, uncrowned political king of New Mexico Territory.

Trailing the rest of the county in population, education, political standards and economic growth, the Territory had four solid assets: lots of land, cattle, a growing network of railroads and rich mines. Dishonest politics created opportunity for those interested and who had money. As the word spread, opportunists flocked into the Territory.

Only months after his arrival Catron learned that political success also led to wealth, that much of the wealth was in land, and most of the land was in Mexican hands. To begin acquiring all three, he first formed a law firm, then a loose network of resourceful individuals with flexible ethics informally known as the "Santa Fe Ring." At one time or another Catron's law firm was said to have employed half of the Territory's future attorneys general and chief justices. He had many enemies, but no friend ever thought of abandoning his allegiance to Tom Catron. Nor would he let them.

Said to be the owner of nearly three million acres, Catron wanted to add the plum of La Constancia as a vacation home. When he heard of Otero's death, he shrewdly guessed that the widow and her daughter would be confused and vulnerable to pressure. So he summoned his favorite heavy lifter, Camp Brown. He looked up from his desk.

"Cancel anything you've got to do for the next couple of weeks. I've got an assignment for you that's going to take a little while.

"Say, Brown, on and off you've been working for about six years, haven't you?"

Pretty sporadic employment, thought Brown.

"Eight years this September, Mr. Catron."

"I've always paid you for the time you spent on the job, right?"

"Don't think I know what you mean."

Catron pivoted in his chair and snatched a Confederate officer's sword from where it hung on the wall. Withdrawing it from its scabbard, he walked around the desk and suddenly drove the point into the floor between Camp Brown's feet.

Pretending not to be startled, Brown watched with fascination its oscillations.

"What I'm getting at, Brown, is I *really* want the *estancia* south of Tome called 'La Constancia.' You're smart and not too fussy about how you get things done. Get La Constancia for me and it means $5,000 in your pocket. If you don't get it, you're back to $25 a day and expenses."

Catron had spiced his modest Civil War record as an officer in the Confederate artillery with a talent for spotting ability in enlisted men and officers. To fill some idle days he attended a trial in which Camp Brown was accused and acquitted of stealing supplies for resale and of killing a fellow officer in the process. A slick and apparently "fixed" defense got him off. In Brown he detected a brutal kind of talent. He filed the face and name in his long memory.

Brown made a practice of applying his peculiar skills for what he could get in return. Early in the War he had posed as an anti-slavery Jayhawker in order to join the infamous guerilla, William Quantrill, in the orgy of pillaging, killing, raping and torching of Lawrence, Kansas. After the raid he bolted south to escape the net thrown out by the Union Army to catch the raiders.

Brown, an accomplished horseman, next volunteered in the guerilla cavalry of General John Singleton Mosby whose slashing raids on Union forces throughout Virginia matched Brown's ruthless style perfectly.

At war's end he drifted aimlessly west, finding occasional employment by men as hard as himself. After five years he trailed into New Mexico and in one more arrived in Santa Fe. There he rented a room. Unemployed but not broke, he frequented the faro tables at Seenson's, one of ten saloons in a two-block stretch of San Francisco Street, running between Burro and Dead Man's alleys.

The dealer at Brown's table stopped shuffling for a minute and said, "Do you know what that slick son-of-a-bitch "Boss" Catron is accused of doing now?"

A faint bell rang in Brown's had.

"Would that be Thomas Catron?"

"The very one."

Brown leaned forward to listen.

"Remember when Luna ran against Manzanas for delegate to Congress last year? Well, they just found out that Catron got some villages upstate to vote for Luna three or four times, and in Rio Quemado he got two hundred and fifty-seven votes out of thirty-three voters."

There was more; voting sheep and the dear departed in support of deposed governor Axtel for chief justice, and land grants that seemed to grow in acreage when surveyed after being bought for a pittance by Catron or another member of the Ring. Then Brown heard about the Ring's sophisticated style of strong-arming. That really appealed to his taste and talents. An outsider, Brown needed to get inside. In a hand-delivered note to Catron's office, Brown wrote of their meeting years before, and gave him names of his better known post-war "employers." Perhaps, he suggested, he could drop by to renew acquaintances.

Always on the lookout for men with special "talents," Catron had Brown checked out. Several weeks later he sent an answer to Brown's rooming house agreeing to a meeting. Since then, Catron had put Brown's unique combination of muscle and deviousness to use. When not employed by Catron, Brown found other things, mostly illegal, to do.

He watched Catron's sword continue to oscillate between his feet. Just for landing La Constancia — $5,000! That was more money than he had ever seen at one time.

"Tell me more," he said, leaning toward the lawyer.

"Some confusion in La Constancia's title will shortly make it available. Don't let it get on the market. I want it!"

When Catron or the Ring were involved in real estate, Brown noticed there was always "confusion" about the land titles.

"Otero's widow and daughter live there. Tell them you'll pay a good deal of money for the *estancia*. If that doesn't work, use your imagination to persuade them that selling would be in *their* best interests."

CHAPTER 19

AS HE APPROACHED the front gate of La Constancia, Martín was appalled at the number of carriages and saddle horses jamming the hitchrail. Inside the wall strangers were examining the house's exterior in detail, picking fruit from the small orchard as if the house was empty. No one came out to greet him or take his horses.

He found a spot at the cluttered hitchrail to wrap Pizarra's reins. The bay he left tethered to the wagon. The strangers continued to ignore him. Pulling the rifle out of its scabbard with a flourish and plenty of noise, he strode toward the double gate of the *zaguan* and pounded on it with his rifle butt.

Only then did the strangers turn to look. A man in city clothes brushed his shoulder and glared as he passed. Martín's cold blue eyes met his. Embarrassed, the man sped out the gate. The pounding on the mesquite door finally persuaded a reluctant Tranquilo Villareal to open the small door in the big gate. His worried look turned into a smile of relief and genuine welcome as he saw Martín's tall figure.

"*Pase usted, por favor,* señor Martín!"

In don Manuel's office sat Catalina and her mother, the strain, worry and fatigue of recent weeks mirrored in their faces. One look at Martín and Catalina tried to smile, then sobbing, ran and buried her face on his chest. Martín raised her chin.

Mi cara! Things can't be that bad!"

Catalina looked up at him with a misty smile. Tears of relief flowed unchecked down doña Margarita's cheeks. She ran over and clung to Martín, too. An embarrassed Tranquilo stood in the doorway.

"*Que pasa aqui,* señora? All those men outside. Who are they?" he asked.

Doña Margarita concealed her wet face with both hands as she sat down heavily.

In a weary monotone she said, "Someone in Santa Fe is questioning the validity of the La Constancia grant. Something to do about not recording or re-recording the original grant of the *estancia,* I'm not sure which."

She wept again, this time with frustration and anger. After a deep breath to compose herself, she continued.

"La Constancia was granted to my husband's family about a hundred years ago. It seems odd that the only question of ownership I've ever heard should occur within weeks of Manuel's death.

"Now those real estate jackals are snooping around. I suppose trying to figure out what the *estancia* is worth. It's as if we didn't live here. It's like they're sniffing at something already dead."

So that was the "pressure from Santa Fe" Carlos mentioned in his note.

"Stop worrying about the 'jackals,' " said Martín. "I think they'll be happy to leave shortly."

With rifle in hand he walked determinedly down the *zaguan.* Who could be behind this flurry of activity? The state or private interests? Probably the latter. He vaguely remembered his father talking about a group called the "Santa Fe Ring" and their obsession with land. Aaron said they seemed to hover wherever ownership was in dispute. La Constancia's prime acreage and several miles of river front certainly made it a target for land-hungry buyers.

Before stepping out of the mouth of the passageway, Martín paused to let his eyes adjust to the light. Between the *hacienda* and its surrounding wall were a half dozen men. One had even climbed onto the tile roof of the *portal* surrounding the patio to describe what he could see of the patio and house. They didn't notice Martín.

With his rifle pointed straight up, he squeezed the trigger. At the muzzle blast there was dead silence. All heads swiveled in his direction.

"Off this property," he said in a loud voice. "Anyone who comes back I'll shoot as a trespasser. You on the *portal,* break one tile on your way down and I'll break your arm."

There was a mass exodus toward the front gate. The man on the *portal* roof, as startled as the rest, scrambled backward, fell heavily, then limped away.

Only Camp Brown did not leave. Tall, beefy, a scar running from behind his left ear to the corner of his mouth, Brown crossed his arms and stared cockily at Martín with what was intended to be a menacing look.

"I represent Thomas B. Catron of Santa Fe and I want to talk to you."

"Never heard of Thomas B. Catron of Santa Fe. Don't care if you represent the governor. I've no interest in talking to you. Get going!"

Always the intimidator, Brown had never been spoken to like that. Considering the stakes, he hesitated, then used a more conciliatory tactic. With an obviously forced smile and hand extended, he said, "My name is Camp Brown. I'm sure glad you got rid of those others so we could talk about selling La Constancia."

Martín ignored the hand.

"This place is not for sale, and you have exactly one minute to leave."

Brown turned ugly again.

"You greaser son-of-a-bitch, I'll be back. You can count on that!"

Martín didn't change his expression.

"If you come back, don't count on one minute."

Brown joined the others, many shaking their fists and

cursing him.

In a high-pitched voice one man yelled, "I don't know who you are, but I'll be back with a title to this place. You look like a stupid greaser to me. You can't tell us what to do!"

Martín laughed. "I just did."

He knew he had done the easy part. These men or worse might return. Back in the office Catalina and her mother, who had been watching from the window, rewarded him with looks of relief. He hadn't returned to La Constancia to chase away real estate men, but the women's relief and gratitude almost made his trip back worthwhile.

Look as they might, neither the original grant nor its re-recording could be found. That problem couldn't be solved by a rifle shot. Martín knew little about the law. But from Mexican friends who had found out the hard way by losing their property, he learned the first rule of land grants: make sure they are properly recorded.

Otero's meticulous father would certainly have re-recorded the original grant as required by the Americans a decade after they took over New Mexico Territory. Somewhere in the *hacienda* there had to be copies. But where? The original deed from the Spanish Crown was probably lost somewhere in Mexico City's voluminous file of ancient documents.

Had someone in Santa Fe made the Territory's copy disappear? Its disappearance was probably the reason for all the real estate activity. The Oteros needed legal help for sure. If there was one competent, honest lawyer in Santa Fe, Sheriff John Bartlett in Belen would probably know.

By rope ferry across the Rio Grande and then on to Belen was only four miles. The morning after his arrival at La Constancia, Martín rode along the river under the cottonwoods and through willow thickets, a refreshing contrast to the dry, dusty roads of the valley.

He had almost reached the rope ferry at the southern boundary of the *estancia* when a rifle shot sheared off a heavy limb inches above his head. Startled, tangled in the leafy end of the branch, he flung himself back in the saddle instinctively pulling on the reins. Pizarra reared, pirouetted and slipped off the bank into the river. Unhorsed, Martín took a few strokes to the bank and climbed out, dripping, He heard the rifleman gallop away, frightened off by three riders leaving the ferry at its western terminus. Who in God's name had fired at him, he wondered. Some hothead from the group of real estate men he had chased off?

Shaken, he continued down to the ferry, crossed the river and trotted into Belen. The tall, stout sheriff grinned and stuck out his big hand when they met again.

"Howdy, Martín. Good to see you. You look a bit damp. Not in trouble again, are you?"

Martín shrugged.

"Hope not. I think Quarai was my last big adventure."

Two windows flanked the door to Bartlett's office, a room scarcely large enough for his oversize frame. On the wall behind his well-worn desk hung a full gun rack: rifles, carbines, shotguns, pistols in leather holsters. His chair protested as he sat down and motioned Martín into the only other one. Bartlett crossed his feet on the desk, tilted his chair back and laced his hands behind his head.

"Gotta say thanks for cleaning out that bunch of rustling *Tejanos*. Shore rattled a lot of stockmen over in the valley. Those three punks we brung back most likely'll swing. If they don't, they'll be in the Santa Fe *juzgado* for one long spell. Guess that ain't why yore here though."

Martín got right to the point.

"Any honest lawyers in Santa Fe?"

To make certain the sheriff would not think it was his own problem, he quickly added, "The Otero women need help."

Guardedly, Bartlett replied, "What kind?"

"Someone who can handle a challenge to a land title."

"You talkin' about Otero's spread? That nice lady and her pretty daughter? Can't believe anyone would want to challenge *their* title. Oteros been there near a hunnert years. Those ladies done more for folks in these river towns than any dozen families I could name. Guess you wouldn't be askin' if you weren't needin'. Let me think about it. Comin' up with the name of an honest lawyer in Santa Fe ain't easy."

The sheriff got up ponderously, walked over to the open window and spat, then returned to his seat. Bartlett's openness and willingness to help a Mexican surprised Martín, especially as he had caused the sheriff a lot of trouble.

Encouraged, Martín added, "The women and I were pretty upset by those real estate hombres swarming over the *hacienda*. Don't know where they're from, but they must think the place will be up for sale soon, or that the Oteros are too naive to know what they're doing."

"Real estate men? Any of 'em say they're from Santa Fe?"

"I'm sure one was. Why?"

"Ever hear of the Santa Fe Ring? Did he mention Tom Catron?"

"Damn if he didn't."

"That's Catron for ya! If land's involved, he'll lead his buzzards through the smallest crack in the law to get it. You're shore goin' to need a lawyer. There's got to be a copy of the grant deed somewhere in the *hacienda*.

The Otero women have been tearing it apart looking for it."

"Could be somebody's pulled the territory's copy out of the records in Santa Fe and hopes that in the confusion the Otero women will sell out. Be just like Catron!

"Martín, next time you get visitors you don't want, send somebody. Don't care who's on the property. I'll put the fear a' God in 'em."

After repeated thanks and several handshakes, Martín left and rode back to La Constancia to report his conversation with Bartlett. At suppertime a rider from Belen delivered a short note.

"Here's the name of somebody in Santa Fe you can trust — Charlie Fiske. I'm wiring him you'll be there in a couple of days. Good luck. J.B."

Next morning Martín tried systematizing the women's search for the deeds. The logic of its being in the office was compelling. But considering the modifications to the *hacienda* over the years, it could be anywhere. Secret drawers, hollowed-out furniture components, mended upholstery, patched or re-plastered adobe, all were candidates for searching.

Before leaving for Santa Fe, he cautioned the women and Tranquilo that pressure from real estate people could continue.

"Don't let anyone in until I get back."

CHAPTER 20

AT NOON Martín left La Constancia. On Pizarra he took the road north toward Albuquerque and the train that would get him to Santa Fe where he hoped Fiske could help him find the original deed.

He still felt guilt over killing Baird. Even more so, the rider at the mission. Besides Catalina's reactions, he needed another sounding board. Immediately he thought of Father Ralliere, the priest who buried Manuel Otero and whose school he had attended. Why not stop and talk to him on the way to Albuquerque?

* * * * *

In New Mexico grapes were harvested in early September. At Tome, Martín found Ralliere in his tiny vineyard cutting off and dropping cones of them into woven willow baskets.

"Father, I need to talk to you. Or rather I need you to talk to me."

Ralliere wiped his hands and smiled.

"I'm embarrassed. My small fiesta is coming up shortly, and here you catch me picking grapes to make wine for the one next year."

Around Tome Ralliere was criticized for his strong stands on many community issues. Even more irksome to the pious were his yearly fiestas for other priests in the diocese. To Ralliere the fiesta was an opportunity to exchange views with clerics who had little exposure to the real world. Most lived by directives from diocese headquarters in Santa Fe. Few took the chance to think for themselves. Laymen thought the fiestas were licentious.

The affairs were highlighted with wine from Ralliere's vineyard and celebrated with singing, card playing and pissing contests, all in all, a modest effort to help relieve the priests' year-long isolation.

"I know you didn't come here to talk about the delicious fruits of my labor, though I'm quite proud of this year's crop. Let's go inside."

"I'll give your next year's fiesta a helping hand."

Muscular Martín scooped up the brimming baskets and carried them into a small storage room where the grapes were cooled before being pressed.

Once inside the priest's spartan parlor, Martín blurted out his dilemma.

"Father, I'm troubled not only by what's happened already, but what may happen. In the past weeks I've killed two men, one in self-defense, I've told myself. The other I rationalized was in defense of my wounded father. Neither man *had* to die. Both deaths were the result of my passion, not reason. The men were also *gringos*."

Ralliere quietly said, "I know of both of these."

Martín pressed on. "What worries me is that I may have become indifferent to another's death, especially if they're *gringos*. Suppose I find myself in the same position again?"

"My answer may surprise but not satisfy you. I live in two worlds: the Church's and the one in which we, here in Tome, in the Territory, endure daily. Do you have any idea what conflicting perspectives these two worlds give me? In one is the perfection demanded by the Church. In the other is the reality of the way people think and act. Like you, for instance."

Ralliere got to his feet, went to a cupboard, reached in and took out a sheathed saber, blew off accumulated dust, and slowly pulled it from its scabbard.

"I've not always been a priest. When a young man, I went to St. Cyr, a French military academy founded, ironically enough, in an abandoned convent. The night of our graduation I went drinking with classmates. We all had too much wine. Believing I had insulted him, one of my classmates tried to kill me. I killed him first with this sword."

Astounded, Martín couldn't take his eyes off Ralliere.

"Self-defense," he smiled wryly, "won me an acquittal. There were many witnesses. But I was dismissed from the Service. Oddly, I went on to my second choice for a career, the priesthood. The military and the Church. Interesting bedfellows, don't you think?

"I never washed that man's blood off my sword. It's there to remind me how closely life and death are intertwined."

Slowly exhaling, Martín said, "You're the only priest I've ever met who's a realist."

"Reality has been forced on me. Our world here is brutal, sometimes almost brutish, always greedy. Many of its victims, mostly Mexicans, are the poorest and least able to bear the pain."

Ralliere fell silent. Martín needed an answer to another question.

"Aren't many of the Mexican's problems caused by the attitude of *gringos?* Dark skin seems to make many Anglo-Americans think Mexicans are inferior, uneducated, lacking in ambition or initiative. Their being Catholic makes it even worse."

"Yes and no," answered Ralliere. "Most Anglo-Americans in the East live in their own world of prejudice: demeaning blacks; distrusting Irish, Poles, Italians; denigrating the Jews. Those that moved West brought all their biases with them and found a handy new target, the Mexican. It'll take more time than we have, but eventually the Anglo-American will learn they're not superior. Let's not pile our prejudices on top of theirs.

"Besides being brutal, many people here are selfish and greedy. But without being tough, how can one survive in a huge, hard, almost empty land? The mere needs of survival toughen you. Selfishness is just a survival technique. Mexican and Anglos are both guilty. Greed is another way to survive. We see it mostly in lust for land. Livestock, too. But it starts with the land."

"You're sure right about land, Father. Fighting for it caused Otero's death."

"An admirable man. He sought to protect both land and livestock. The hidden motive, I suspect, not even recognized by don Manuel, was greed disguised by right of possession. And look at the death of your friend Kusz."

Ralliere stood up and smiled.

"Maybe you should have asked me only one question — about the sanctity of life, eh?"

He slid the sword into the scabbard, put both back in the cupboard, and turned to look at Martín.

"I hear you're getting married."

"I certainly want to. First we've got to resolve the status of La Constancia. Can you imagine that the Oteros' ownership is being questioned simply because no one can find the deed?"

As Ralliere sat down again, he said with an air of innocence, "Tell me honestly, Martín. Which attracts you more: Catalina Otero or the possibility of becoming the new *patron* of the *estancia?*"

"I was in love with Catalina even before her father was killed and would have taken her anywhere just to be with her. No one, Father, and I guess that means doña Margarita and her brother Carlos, has talked about offering me a job at La Constancia. In fact, doña Margarita has Carlos looking in Santa for a professional manager."

"Let's have some sandwiches and coffee," said Ralliere. "Suppertime seems to have slipped right by us."

In his tiny kitchen Ralliere sliced breast meat from a chicken, added wood to the stove, put water on to boil, then warmed a half-dozen *tortillas* on the still-glowing coals of the *comal*. Into each *tortilla* he folded the chicken and a spoonful of *chile con carne,* then returned to the living room with a heaping plate.

"Coffee will be ready in five minutes."

Between bites Martín said, "Father, you've given me more answers than I know what to do with."

"At your age everyone wants perfect answers and solutions. I'm surprised you feel so strongly about not killing. Many of the men I meet view the death of others with indifference because they think themselves to be immortal. That's why we send young men to fight our wars."

"What do I do if I'm forced to make another decision between life and death?"

"It's easy for me to tell you to shoot only to wound if you have to shoot at all. Yet, will there always be time for rational decisions? From personal experience I know the strength of the instinct for self-preservation. If the law hasn't condemned you for what you've already done, how can I? As a priest, I spend much time trying to equate my concern for human life with the realities of life here."

It was late. Both yawned. Martín said goodnight and bedded down on the small pallet provided by Ralliere. For the first time in weeks he slept without violent dreams. Up at dawn, he saddled Pizarra and headed for Albuquerque to catch the morning train to Santa Fe.

CHAPTER 21

THOUGH BACK IN SANTA FE, Camp Brown hadn't dared report to Catron that things weren't going well in getting his hands on La Constancia. Anxious for news on progress, Catron strode into his office and yelled for someone, anyone, to find Brown. The bullied employees again scurried aimlessly, while the same alert clerk as before went straight to Camp's boarding house to find him in bed badly hung over. Brown's excuse to himself for drinking was the need for self-composure before reporting his initial failure. He did not want to face Catron with the lame excuse that a greaser had prevented him from succeeding.

Now, over-composed, he was called to report. Bleary-eyed, Brown appeared in Catron's office to find the man boiling with his usual impatience.

Though Catron suspected what the answer would be, he said, "What progress have you made?"

Brown shuffled his feet and stammered, "There's a lot of competition for the property. Real estate people are all over it. Some greaser with a rifle came out of the *hacienda* and threw us all out. Even I couldn't get in."

"Don't tell me about your problems," Catron barked and looked hard at Camp. "I can't tolerate failure, yours or anybody else's. Goddammit, I told you to use your imagination. I really don't care how you do it, just bring me La Constancia!"

* * * * *

Much earlier that morning Martín quick-walked Pizarra the twenty miles from Tome to Albuquerque. He left him at the livery stable across from the depot and boarded the 9:00 AM for a rainy, two-hour trip to Lamy. There he transferred to the three-coach spur line train into nearby Santa Fe. As he stepped out of the coach, a broiling sun emerged to welcome him.

Across from the newly built Chapel of Loretto, a block south of Santa Fe's central plaza, Charlie Fiske waited in his law office for the new client, something of a rarity for the young lawyer. Smoke from his strong Mexican cigar drifted out the open window and down the narrow hallway. Through the open door he saw and sized up his approaching visitor. As Martín entered, Fiske stubbed out the cigar and with a broad grin stuck out his hand. The return smile and equally firm grip started their meeting off well.

"Charlie Fiske is my name, but I'd appreciate your just calling me 'Charlie.'"

Shortly, it became clear to Martín that Fiske was one of the few attorneys in town untainted by the Ring. He despised what it was doing to Mexican land owners and the reputation of the Territory. Martín's visit turned out to be more educational than productive. Land law was Fiske's specialty, and he knew what it took to get results from the labyrinthine New Mexican court system.

"Got to be honest with you, Martín. Political leverage, connections and money count here. I've got none of them. But without having the original grant in their hands or a fair copy, the Oteros don't have a lot of options. I'll ransack the court files, and I hope they tear that *hacienda* apart, too."

"They're already doing that."

Fiske walked over to the window and watched a burro loaded with charcoal skirt the plaza. Arms crossed, he turned and looked at Martín.

"Give the United States some credit. After the war with

Mexico the treaty of Guadalupe Hidalgo was an honest attempt by the U.S. to protect property and other rights of the Mexican majority. The treaty's a little murky on details, one of the reasons the Ring's been so successful. About land, in essence it says that if you can *prove* title to a Spanish or Mexican land grant, it'll be recognized."

"Charlie, their grant's *got* to be valid. Nobody's challenged it for almost a hundred years."

"I'm sure you're right, but some Mexicans were pretty lax about recording, or hid their copies generations ago. Descriptions of property lines were often vague, like being between trees, rocks or springs that no longer exist or can't be identified."

Fiske sat down.

"In the mid-fifties a Surveyor General was appointed to re-record and reaffirm all grants. The necessity of doing this was heavily advertised. Otero's father must have re-recorded his deed."

"I hate to say it, but if the Ring's interested in the property, Catron could have had the deed misfiled or removed, but not destroyed. Sooner or later he'd need it to prove ownership. None of this is much help, but at least now you know about as much as I do."

Charlie leaned forward with a smile. "How about a beer, Martín? Might be the most helpful thing we could do right now."

"Inspired idea, Charlie. I accept."

The bar at the Exchange Hotel across from the corner of the plaza was almost cool. Their first beer begged for another. Fiske talked about Santa Fe history and told amusing local anecdotes of which he seemed to know an endless number. For the first time in days Martín laughed. Two frock-coated customers, looking like the politicians they probably were, got up to leave, having drunk more than enough, and stopped close to Wolf's table.

Loud enough to be heard by most patrons, one said, "Sam, d'you s'pose there's a sheepherder convention in town?"

Heads pivoted.

Sam said, "Sure smells like it. Did I tell you about the new use greasers found for sheep? Wool!" Doubled over, he slapped his leg in appreciation of his wit.

Fiske jumped to his feet, but Martín pulled him down and leaned casually back in his chair.

In meticulous English he said, "That story's about five years old. It wasn't funny then, either."

Everyone heard Martín. Many laughed. A few even nodded approval. The look in his blue eyes was more than enough for the politicos. Both weaved quickly out of the bar.

Fiske smiled and said, "Nicely handled. Lost my head. The Oteros are lucky to have you around."

"I'm practicing getting used to people like that."

Fiske paid for the beer and led his client outside to see the limited sights of Santa Fe. Later, they parted with a handshake, Fiske promising again to search the archives.

Impatient to get back to La Constancia, Martín went to bed early in his simple rooming house so he could catch the first train to Lamy and then go on to Albuquerque. In growing morning heat he walked to the station past blocks of graceless adobes lining the town's dirt streets. On the ride back he thought through what he had learned from Fiske. Nothing helpful. Unless the Oteros found a copy of the deed and its re-recording, their future looked dim.

* * * * *

In a rented buggy Camp Brown headed south from Albuquerque to La Constancia. He had rehearsed his plan to insinuate his way into a meeting with the Otero women. At the *estancia* he persuaded a very reluctant Villareal that he might have a solution to the Oteros' problems. Despite Martín's warning, doña Margarita agreed to talk, hoping desperately to find out more about the problems facing them.

Brown's first words were untactful and openly aggressive. "Mrs. Otero, you know there is a real doubt about your ownership of this land. No one can find the original grant or reconfirmation of it in the Santa Fe archives."

Catalina gave Brown a hard look but said nothing.

Angered, her mother answered immediately. "Why should I take your word for anything? It seems extremely odd that after a hundred years of Otero ownership our grant would be questioned only a few weeks after my husband's death."

"I'm not a lawyer, Mrs. Otero, but do represent a man who feels very sorry for your predicament. He's ready to pay twenty-five thousand dollars for everything here."

Doña Margarita took a moment to digest Brown's offer, then steeled herself to answer calmly.

"If we have no legal right to La Constancia, why should your principal pay us anything? Where will *he* find a title? There's something dreadfully wrong about all of this. You know it as well as we do. I don't like you and I'm not interested in your offer. You may leave."

Incensed, she called Tranquilo to hurry Brown out the door. To have the logic of his offer so quickly punctured and dismissed so bluntly, especially by a female greaser, infuriated Brown. Shown out the gate, he grimly began plotting his next move, something that would be sure to bring down the Oteros.

As he climbed into his buggy, still fuming, the idea hit him. Over the years many would have worked at La Constancia and some let go for good reason. As a result, they probably would hold a grudge against the *patron,* justified or not. Malice was a great persuader to get even. Mexican bars in nearby towns might produce some leads to such a person. Dark saloons in Tome, Adelino and La Madera were explored by Brown looking for the right man. He stayed away from Belen, too close to the sheriff. Finally, in the small town of Trujillos his discreet inquiries uncovered a promising candidate — Angel Vigil.

For several years Vigil, a compulsive thief, had worked at La Constancia. After his third theft, even the patient Otero agreed he had to go. Since then Vigil convinced himself that the *patron,* not he, was to blame for putting temptation in his way. Brown found Angel just where he had been told he would, asleep in a crumbling adobe on the edge of Adelino, a minute village just north of La Constancia. Toed awake by Brown, he sleepily agreed to meet him in an hour at the only *cantina* in town.

Barely avoiding the body of a drunk curled into a foetal position, Brown picked his way across the packed dirt floor of the dimly lit bar smelling of urine, spilled tequila and stale beer. In one corner at a sticky fly-blown table sat a raggedly dressed man.

"Is that you, Angel Vigil? Can I buy you a tequila?"

"The answer to both questions is *si,* señor."

Brown picked his way over to the bar, a wood plank supported by the backs of two spread-out chairs, seats anchored with bricks. A woman with iron gray hair in a severe bun and an aggressive look tended bar. On a packing case behind her was a small display of bottles, tequila and aguardiente. She frowned suspiciously at the Anglo until she saw the silver dollar in his palm. American cash was welcome.

Beaming now, she handed him an unopened bottle of tequila and two dirty glasses. Where Vigil sat, Brown wiped off the filthy bench with his handkerchief, polished his glass and sat down. He poured Vigil a generous drink and a short one for himself.

"I understand you're no friend of the Oteros."

"*Correcto* again, señor. I could pees on Otero's grave with joy. May I ask who you are?"

As an answer, in the center of the table Brown mounded silver dollars poured from his leather purse. Slowly he counted out twenty-five of them which he pushed in front of Vigil.

"That's who I am. And they're twenty-five more just like these if you'll do something for me that's very easy."

The mound of silver dollars in front of Vigil took immediate effect. Open-mouthed and wide-eyed, Angel stared at more money than he had ever seen in his life. Mesmerized, he kept his eyes on the silver dollars as if they might disappear.

"Of course, señor, I'll be happy to do anything for you."

Brown leaned back against the filthy adobe wall.

"First, how many wells are there on La Constancia?"

"Three, señor," replied Vigil eagerly. "One for drinking water in the *pueblito* where the workers live, one to water the stock near the barn and corral, and there's another one at the *hacienda*."

"Angel, just north of La Constancia there's a little bridge over the *acequia* that runs into the *estancia*. Know it?"

"Of course, señor."

"Meet me there tomorrow night at midnight, Angel. Midnight *en punto!*"

"Si, señor. I will be happy to see you again at the bridge."

Certain he had picked the right man, Brown smiled to himself and, taking no chances, left the cantina with the bottle of tequila.

CHAPTER 22

MARTÍN SWUNG OFF THE TRAIN as it reached Albuquerque, crossed the street and walked into the livery stable where Pizarra nickered a welcome and pawed the floor of his stall. After scratching the big gray's nose and saddling him, he rode south toward La Constancia at a trot. Catalina heard him ride into the stable and waited at the *zaguan* entrance to greet him, impatient for his arms and news.

Before she could speak, he said, "Any luck?"

Embarrassed to have failed in the search, Catalina looked at the ground.

"No, but we found some interesting papers on family history when the Oteros still lived in Mexico City."

He almost let slip a sarcastic comment, but checked himself and nodded as though interested. At supper Martín described his meeting with Fiske and his confidence in the attorney.

"He says we've absolutely got to find the reconfirmation of the grant. He'll ransack the archives, but he thinks the original document may have been made to temporarily disappear."

Margarita described Camp Brown's unpleasant visit. Startled, Martín looked at her in disbelief. "I thought you weren't going to let anyone in!"

"I'm sorry, Martín, we just had to know what kind of a problem we had."

"That man works for Tom Catron, the head of what's called the 'Santa Fe Ring.' He and Brown *son malos hombres.* There's no telling *what* Brown will do to get his hands on this place."

All three fell silent. Proof of ownership was the only answer.

* * * * *

Just before midnight Camp Brown crossed the crude wood bridge over the *acequia* that ran into La Constancia. He stopped the buggy. From under its seat he pulled three twenty-five-pound, tightly woven cloth sacks and dumped them on the edge of the road. Carefully, he rinsed his hands in the *acequia*, then drove the rig off the road into a clump of piñon. Even further from the road he picketed the horse.

Anticipating a long wait, he lighted a cigar, cupping its glow between his hands. To his surprise, shortly after midnight Angel Vigil materialized out of the dark. Didn't know greasers could tell time, he thought to himself.

"Here I am as you asked, señor."

Keep instructions simple was Brown's hallmark. "Angel, here are three full sacks. Pour what's in 'em, one full sack into each well on La Constancia. Be back here in an hour and a half. When you're finished, you'll get twenty-five more silver dollars. To get the money you must bring back the cloth bags, empty. All three of them. *Comprende?* He counted on Vigil's hatred of Otero to do the job right.

To make certain he added, "If the powder is not put in the wells, I'll know about it tomorrow and you'll be very, very sorry."

As to the risk of handling the contents, well, that was Angel's lookout. Vigil knew Brown meant what he said.

"Do not worry, señor, it will be done as you ask."

In what little starlight there was, Brown saw Vigil smile. In anticipation of the task or the reward? Vigil nodded once again and asked no questions. Brown helped him shoulder the seventy-five-pound load and watched him climb awkwardly over the fence and disappear into the darkness.

Vigil could not read. If he could, he would have seen that the labels printed on the sacks read "WOLF AND COYOTE BAIT." Printed in red below and underlined were the words "DANGER — ARSENIC — POISON." And for Mexican users the words "PELIGRO — ARSENICA — VENEMO." One sack would normally last a rancher a couple of years. Brown, as usual, took no chances. That Vigil couldn't read the label made no difference, he already knew what he was about to do.

The nearest well was at the kitchen end of the *hacienda*. Moving easily along the outside of the six-foot-high adobe wall enclosing the building, Vigil was also screened by piñon trees and overgrown chamisa bushes. The wall made it impossible for anyone inside the *hacienda* to see him or hear his occasional stumble. At the west end of the *hacienda* the wall stopped. The section running at right angles to it had been pulled down. He could see the kitchen door and the location of the well from the outline of its pulley frame. Cautiously he looked into the kitchen window. The lantern always burning there revealed no one. He crawled to the well head and dropped the heavy sacks from his shoulder. With his clasp knife he slit open one end, then poured its contents into the well. The job was done carefully and soundlessly. On the next leg his burden would be twenty-five pounds lighter.

Each well on the *estancia* had been dug about the same size, three feet in diameter and twenty-five feet deep. Water seeped into them through sandy channels dug from the Rio Grande. The wells were designed to provide at least ten feet of clear stored water and five for settling. Camp Brown knew what he was doing. Twenty-five pounds of pure arsenic in that small volume of water would create a fatal brew.

Cautiously, Vigil retraced his path to the front of the *hacienda*, turned south, moving slowly just outside the building's front wall. Ahead of him he could see the outline of the *estancia's* bulky barn. He knew approximately where the stock well should be, found it, cut open the second sack and poured in its contents.

Riskiest would be the last well, the one that served the *pueblito*. A half-mile south of the barn, the well was centered in a minute *plaza*. Vigil knew that at any time during the night water might be drawn by a sleepless inhabitant. With extra caution he approached the *plaza*. No lights shown from any of the small adobe dwellings. Vigil slithered on his stomach to the well, keeping his head below its stone rim. Into the *pueblito's* only source of drinking water he poured the contents of the last sack of arsenic.

Turning east, he scurried in a crouch across the fields and to the road along the edge of the *estancia*. Once over the fence, he threw himself on the ground to catch his breath. In minutes he was up and dog-trotting north to the rendezvous with Brown and his hard-earned twenty-five dollars. Suddenly he remembered.

"I'm supposed to bring back three sacks," he muttered to himself. Only two were in his hand. He panicked.

"The third! Did I drop it along the road? No, I must have left it at one of the wells."

Angry, frustrated, he hit his forehead with the heel of his hand and said, *"Dios! Que es!"*

Too chancy to re-enter the *estancia* now. He would have to bluff it out with the *gringo* Brown who would probably not even notice the missing sack. Besides, by the stars he knew it was close to two in the morning, later than he was expected back. To Vigil's relief, the man was still there, hands cupped around his third cigar, inhaling nervously.

"Did you do it?"

"Of course, señor."

He threw himself down next to Brown, covering the two sacks with his body, panting from his long trot up the road.

"It is finished. All three wells." The words popped out of his mouth before he could stop himself.

"You're late. Thought you were in trouble" Pulling the two bags from under Vigil, Brown snapped, "Where's the third?"

"It's not there?" said Vigil, feigning surprise. "I must have dropped it along the road."

"Go back and get it. Three bags or no twenty-five silver dollars."

Never having dreamed of so much money, Vigil knew he couldn't afford to lose it. Down the dark dirt road he disappeared, resigned, certain now the bag was at the stock well. Opposite where he thought the barn should be, Vigil slipped through the fence and headed west across the meadow at a furtive run. The barn and the well-head frame were dimly outlined by starlight. Vigil covered the last few yards with a rush, dropped to his knees and began feeling frantically for the telltale sack.

He had already been spotted. A worker sleeping in the barn as a guard had been alarmed by a small noise and the shadowy figure of Vigil's first intrusion. Vigil was on his way to the little pueblo while the man ran to wake Tranquilo Villareal at the *hacienda*.

With a partially shuttered bull's eye lantern the two first searched the barn, then around the corral. Nothing suspicious. Between barn and corral was the well. On the second pass by the well the toe of the mayordomo's boot caught on the cloth bag. In the narrow ray of the lantern he read the words "Wolf and Coyote Bait" and instantly guessed what had happened. He snapped the lantern shut.

His mouth went dry as he sucked in his breath, his pulse raced and he murmured, *"Por Dios!* He must have poisoned all three wells!"

Uncomprehending, the worker stared at Tranquilo in silence. At the sound of running both men tensed. Vigil's frustration made him careless. On his knees in the high grass near the well, he swung his arms back and forth like a scythe in a frantic search for the sack. Knee driving hard his kidney, Tranquilo hit him viciously from behind. The air exploded from Angel's lungs. The worker grabbed and quickly tied the prostrate Vigil's arms tightly behind him. In the full light of the open lantern Tranquilo was surprised to see who it was. He himself had thrown Vigil off the *estancia* the previous year.

In a low, tense voice Villareal said, "Angel Vigil! What could you be doing here? Are you looking for something? Perhaps this?" shoving the sack empty of its deadly contents directly into Vigil's face.

The man flinched, struggling fruitlessly.

In the same controlled voice he continued, "I think you have made a bad mistake here, Angel. I hope you have not done so elsewhere on La Constancia."

At that moment, magnified by the night air, from the direction of the little pueblo came the wail of a woman in an agony of sorrow. In moments angry voices followed, growing in volume as more people wakened. Only Vigil knew what the cry meant, and silently cursed himself again for returning. By a rope around his neck he was led to the small pueblo like a dog and tied tightly to a deeply planted fence post.

In almost every home lighted kerosene lanterns showed dimly through scraped hide glazing, but people clustered around only one. Villareal pushed through the crowd around its doorway. Inside, sobbing in gasps, tears cascading down her face, a young woman knelt on the dirt floor. She held to her cheek the limp form of her baby daughter which she rocked helplessly back and forth. Just as stunned, weeping also, the father held the inert body of his dead son.

"I killed them both!" he groaned.

Tranquilo crossed himself, and of no one in particular asked, "How did this terrible thing happen?"

Behind him a man whispered, "The baby girl woke, feverish. Concepcion sent Fermin to the well for water. The girl drank part of a dipper, then the little boy wanted some. In moments both vomited, had stomach cramps and running bowels. They choked, couldn't breathe and, *Madre de Dios*, died."

Villareal seized his informant by his shirt.

"Quick! The well's been poisoned. Cut the bucket from the rope and throw both into the well. Wash your hands in the *acequia*, then guard the well so no one can use it."

He grabbed another man. "Find something to ride. As fast as you can, go to the well at the kitchen end of the *hacienda*. Cut the rope and throw it and the bucket in. Then wake señor Martín. Tell him what's happened. We need him here." Before the man could leave, Tranquilo quickly added, "Afterwards go to the well at the barn and throw in its bucket and rope, too."

Hastily dressed, Martín arrived on the same burro used by the messenger.

Tranquilo gestured toward Angel lashed to the fence post. "We caught the man who did this terrible thing."

He described Vigil's sorry history at La Constancia and how they had surprised him searching for the sack at the barn.

"Angel had twenty-five silver dollars in his pocket. Someone smarter and certainly much richer than he must have put him up to it."

Martín had a suspicion who that might be. "I'll send somebody for the sheriff."

"No, no. Please, señor Martín. This is a village matter. It must be taken care of here."

Martín looked at Villareal, then at the tied figure at the edge of lantern's glow. Once more he had to decide between the life and death of a man.

"Why me?" The words just slipped out.

Though not caught in the act, Vigil had not denied his guilt. If turned over to the sheriff, Bartlett would send Vigil to Santa Fe for trial where both his case and he would be quickly disposed of. If left up to the people in the *pueblito*, justice would be summary and the result the same. Without Vigil, on the other hand, there was no way to identify or implicate Brown, or whoever was behind this terrible act. Aware that he was trying to rationalize his way out of making a decision, another wrenching cry from the children's mother made the choice even harder.

"Tranquilo, without Vigil it will be almost impossible to

identify the man who put him up to this. Can't you make the people here understand that?"

The men of the pueblo were adamant. Any justice other than what they could deal out to Angel Vigil on the spot did not interest them.

"Before they do anything, at least I've got to talk to Angel. Maybe I can convince him to tell who's behind this awful thing," gesturing helplessly toward the well.

He couldn't oppose the community will, and he knew he had just tacitly consented to whatever justice they might mete out. Terrified, Vigil was untied from the post and led to the center of the tiny plaza. By lantern light Martín stared at him with eyes devoid of expression. How could a man hate enough to deliberately kill others he did not know? Martín tried to keep the fury out of his voice.

"I must tell you, Angel, your future appears very uncertain. Every person here is extremely angry with you. I think it's fair they should decide what happens to you, don't you?"

"*Si, señor.*" Then in panic, "I mean no, *señor.*"

Trembling violently, Angel fell on his knees. Eyes bulging with fear, he looked at the stony faces within the circle of dim light, then up at Martín. No mercy there, either.

"I understand you are anxious to make a gift to Fermin and his wife, the ones whose babies died drinking the water you poisoned."

Martín's voice was almost flat.

"Oh, *si,* señor Wolf. There is money in my left pocket. Please give it to my friend Fermin with my deepest sympathy. If I'd only known." He dropped his head as if in sorrow. "There's no way I would have harmed those dear little children."

"But you did, Angel."

Martín reached into Vigil's filthy pocket and pulled out a handful of silver dollars.

"This is, of course, all you have?"

"How stupid of me. I forgot. There's more in my other pocket."

Vigil's ingratiating smile sickened Martín.

"Please, señor Wolf, give it all to Fermin. Oh, those poor adorable babies!"

In hopes his performance was having a positive effect on Martín, he added tears.

"Now, Angel, I know you're going to tell me who gave you those sacks of poison and all that money."

Trembling, Vigil knew this was his last chance to help himself, but could contribute little.

"I don't know, señor. That's God's truth. The man did not tell me his name. I met him in Juanito's *cantina* in Adelino yesterday. He wore a city suit. You know, pants and coat alike, and a round city hat. He was tall and somewhat fat."

That's Brown all right, thought Martín.

"He drove a horse and buggy. Met me at midnight on the little bridge where the *acequia* flows into La Constancia." He turned pleading eyes up to Martín. This time genuine tears were on his face. *"En nombre de Dios,* turn me over to the sheriff, not to these people."

"The sheriff will only see to it that you are hanged quickly. I was wrong, Angel. Your future *is* certain. The people here will decide."

Vigil crawled toward him in a last appeal for mercy. Martín turned away. Rudely jerked to his feet by one of the men, the whimpering Vigil was again tied to the post. It was almost dawn.

"Tranquilo, please have someone saddle Pizarra immediately and bring him here. I'll need the saddle scabbard and my Winchester, too."

Then he walked to the desolate couple's small adobe, searching for words to ease their sorrow. Beyond the fact they were still young, he could think of none. Without comment he placed the silver dollars on the sheet iron grill of the *comal.* He turned to express his deep sorrow for their loss, and the certainty they would have many more lovely children.

By the light of the lantern in the small plaza, Martín could see Pizarra, disturbed by the dark and unfamiliar figures, pawing the ground. He mounted and, as rapidly as darkness permitted, headed for the bridge across the *acequia* into La Constancia. He had only a faint hope that Brown would still be there.

When Vigil disappeared into the *estancia* again to find the missing sack, Camp Brown waited nervously, glancing repeatedly at his watch by the glow of his cigar. Hell, it shouldn't take him more than a half-hour to find that bag. Maybe it was a mistake to send him back. Forty-five minutes later Brown's nerve and patience gave out. He had heard nothing, but he guessed Vigil was in trouble. Quickly hitching the horse to the rented buggy, he headed north toward Albuquerque at a fast trot.

* * * * *

Monsoon season had come in earnest. As far north as one could see, rain clouds were over the Sangre de Cristo range every day at noon. Then came thunder and lightning, followed by curtains of heavy rain reaching far out into the valley, even beyond the Rio Grande. Fed by runoff from streams all along the chain of mountains, the river rose a bit every day. In the cool dampness of early dawn men from the *pueblito* half-dragged, half-carried a protesting Vigil to the river's edge. His hands were lashed below water level to the exposed root of a cottonwood tree and his feet to another, a man's length away. His body was completely submerged, his face still above water. He raged against his captors and the dead Otero, then screamed in terror. Silently, the villagers walked away. The slowly rising Rio Grande would do the rest.

CHAPTER 23

FIRST AT THE TINY PUEBLO, then the *hacienda,* and last at the barn, new wells were quickly and willingly dug. Stock from the barn was temporarily watered at the river. The poisoned old wells were filled with dirt from the new, symbolically burying the tragic past. Fresh adobe walls encircled each new well head and held the wood frame for a pulley, rope and bucket. The Otero women refused to be intimidated by the well poisonings, but Martín warned that Camp Brown would not give up easily.

Shortly after Vigil's disappearance, Sheriff Bartlett and a deputy arrived to see for themselves what had been rumored in Belen to have happened. With genuine sympathy he visited the parents of the tiny victims. No one mentioned Vigil, and Bartlett wisely asked few questions. Martín was certain the sheriff knew or suspected, but decided that whatever its resolution, he had one less problem to handle. The woman bartender in Adelino could only confirm Vigil's description of Brown. In just days Martín found the source of the poison, a feed store in Albuquerque. Its clerk had questioned the size of the purchase, and identified Brown by the description given him.

Meanwhile, at Martín's insistence, room by room the *hacienda* was meticulously rummaged for any document proving the ownership of the Otero grant. Nothing. Gloom deepened with the arrival of an obliquely worded telegram.

It read: "Still searching. C's involvement now certain. Fiske." To disguise his disappointment, Martín took a deep breath and walked out to the patio. Maybe fresh air would clarify his thinking.

In frustration Catalina spun to face her mother. "All this will work out in the end. I just know it! But then we'll be in more trouble with no one to manage La Constancia. You and Uncle Carlos can't find anyone qualified."

Leaning closer, she said forcefully, "This is ridiculous, Mother. We both know Martín's perfectly capable. Look what he's done already, straightened out our accounts, organized the harvest, and now is trying to lead us through this awful mess. Everyone on the *estancia* likes and trusts him. What else do you want? Now's the time he needs encouragement. Tell him he's the new *patron*."

Margarita pressed a handkerchief nervously to her lips and moved uneasily on the sofa. Tears appeared as she shook her head, saying, "I don't know what your father would do."

"Well, I do. He wouldn't hesitate a minute to choose Martín!"

"I guess sadness and this awful predicament is blinding me. You're right, Catalina. Of course, Martín is qualified. Ask him to come in."

Led by Catalina, Martín walked into Otero's office, uneasy, worried that Margarita would start giving him orders. He braced himself.

With a solemn look, Margarita said, "In the midst of all our problems, Martín, this is a very odd time to ask you to consider becoming the new *patron* of La Constancia. Everyone, including myself, has great faith in you."

Startled, at a loss for an appropriate answer, he bowed slightly, managed a weak smile and stammered out, "I accept with thanks, doña Margarita, and I'm truly grateful for your trust in me."

He backed awkwardly onto the patio.

Margarita's clear voice stopped him. "This is not an empty gesture to encourage you, Martín. We need you now, and we'll need you when this is over."

He smiled again. Obviously Catalina had forced the issue. He sat on the broad rim of the patio fountain, pulled both legs up to use his knees as a chin rest. Despite Margarita's confidence in him, he wondered if there'd be a La Constancia to manage.

What should, what could they do? Catron's strategy was clear — intimidate the women by any means. If he was unscrupulous enough to condone well poisoning, what next? Unable to anticipate or prepare against a specific move by Brown, Martín felt relatively helpless. He and Tranquilo were the only men readily available to defend the women. He could not ask for manpower from the little pueblo. Besides, they were hardly range-hardened *vaqueros*. Almost all had wives and children. Martín had confidence in the mayordomo, but how would the women stand up to the kind of pressure Catron could bring to bear?

In an attempt to be positive and constructive, if only to himself, he straightened his back and swung his feet down onto the paving. In General Grant's Civil War memoirs Martín had read an essay on outguessing the enemy. He was no Grant, but Catron and Brown certainly qualified as enemies. The stakes were too high not to think of every possibility. Catron would insulate himself from any rough stuff. Seizing La Constancia required men. Hiring toughs was Brown's kind of job. They couldn't be locals like Vigil, too easily identified. Darkness would be their greatest asset. Brown would have scouted and probably sketched the layout of the *estancia* to fill in his new "employees." Then what would he do? Where would he do it? Not the *pueblito* again, too many people. Nor the *hacienda,* or at least not immediately. Catron would want it intact. That left the barn and corrals. Firing these and destroying stock seemed likely choices.

Would Catron really go to these lengths to get the *estancia?* He had a lot more at stake in the Territory than just picking up another piece of good real estate. Could

Brown be acting on his own, sort of a loose cannon, hoping to ingratiate himself with Catron? That would be even worse.

* * * * *

Martín was close to the truth. Brown knew any hope of becoming a Ring insider hung on his success at getting La Constancia for Catron. He imagined delivering the *estancia* like Salome carrying the head of John the Baptist on a silver salver. Results, not means, counted with Catron. That the well poisoning had killed two children meant nothing to Brown. And he would not send reports back to Santa Fe until he was successful. He hadn't counted on Martín being at the *estancia*. Alone, the women were easy targets. Martín's presence added risk. How much, Brown didn't know. In an effort to find out, he made guarded local inquiries but got few helpful answers. Yes, Wolf had been at Estancia Springs when Otero was killed, but no one knew what role he played. Through a third party Brown even had questions asked at the sheriff's office, hoping to find out what had happened at Quarai. Bartlett's close-mouthed deputies said nothing. They were not being so much discreet as embarrassed by their too-late arrivals at the Springs and then the mission.

Brown knew there was little time. He was sure the original records of the Otero grant in Santa Fe were made to disappear by someone in the Ring. Any moment the women might find Otero's copy at the *hacienda* and spoil his takeover attempt. Especially with Martín at La Constancia, something drastic was needed to make the women submit.

From the bluffs across the road with his binoculars Brown panned every bit of the *estancia*. In a notebook he sketched a detailed map of La Constancia and made copious notes. Further mischief at the little pueblo was out of the question, too many loyal people. Besides, Vigil's sudden disappearance was a bit unnerving, though typical of a greaser. First choices were the barn and corrals. The ancient wood would burn in minutes. Of course, there was always the *hacienda*. Catron would not want it damaged, so that was his last alternative. Maybe it would come to that, but if he had to get to Martín and the women, he could probably break in with little damage.

Until sundown Brown watched the round of activity at La Constancia. Men left the barn in the late afternoon. One stayed behind as a night guard. He was only a greaser and easily taken care of. The *hacienda* hands went to their homes in the evening. But the mayordomo apparently slept at the main house. He was another unknown quantity, but Brown dismissed him as just one more gutless greaser. Did it make a difference that Martín Wolf was part Mexican? He had played a strong hand with his rifle on Brown's first visit. Could he be counted on by the Otero women? He seemed competent, Brown reluctantly admitted, but that didn't mean he could stand up to the kind of pressure Brown planned to bring. He couldn't afford the risk. How to keep Martín from interfering? Better yet, how to get him in the open, get rid of him permanently?

Rounding up anonymous manpower was Brown's first concern. He was good at it. Men of the kind he was looking for were available in the Territory; unemployed, drifting gunmen to whom cash, not conscience, was the criteria. Loyalty went to the high bidder. Race horses run just as well for a new owner. Money was no problem. Brown had plenty. Catron didn't pinch pennies. Two shabby Albuquerque bars provided the men he wanted. He chose three from each. All were strangers to each other — so much the better. All were from out of the Territory and out of work.

Gold double eagles and silver dollars from Brown's seemingly endless supply in a leather grip worked their bright magic. Fifty dollars on the spot, fifty more when the job was completed. Besides money, fear of the huge, aggressive Brown and his ability to control his new employees played their part. Brown's brusque self-confidence made him seem harder than any of them, and they knew it. Besides, Brown's half-truths made the job sound easy; frighten away one man and two women, then be on their way with the rest of their money. Together they poured over Brown's sketch map of the *estancia,* asked a few questions and agreed to meet him at midnight where he had met Vigil. Brown was determined that this time nothing would go wrong.

* * * * *

Martín was franker than he had ever been with the Otero women, wanting them to know what they might be facing this night or in the near future. Catalina would be resilient but tough, he knew. Her mother, he suspected, would also be. Both agreed with his hunches where trouble might start. Both were nervous and fearful.

"Why not send for the sheriff?" Margarita asked. "That's what he's there for."

"I thought about it, even talked to him. He's sympathetic, but wants more proof than I've got that something's going to happen. I couldn't convince him that he and his deputies should stand around here just because we feel uneasy."

To Tranquilo he described where he thought trouble might come. Nothing but determination showed on the mayordomo's face. One more thing to do. Late that evening Martín walked to the barn and talked to the man who was to guard the stock there.

Eyeing his shotgun with misgiving, he said, "If more than one man comes here, leave quietly. Don't shoot."

Then he led Pizarra out of the barn, rode him bareback around to me north side of the *hacienda,* and tethered him to a piñon with a long rope so he could graze.

Feeling a bit foolish, he whispered to the gray, "Whatever happens, don't make a sound."

Any attempt to frighten off Martín and the women, he guessed, would probably be made when they were thought to be asleep. Tranquilo could watch 'til midnight, then he would take over. Every possible preparation he could think of had been made and precaution taken. Sleep overcame him the moment he stretched out on his bed.

Heavy with the promise of rain, the September evening was as sultry as Catalina could remember. At nine, as usual, she went up to her room which, even with the balcony doors flung open, was unbearably humid. Lines of fatigue and beads of perspiration at the roots of her hair were clearly reflected in the mirror. If she looked this tired, what must the strain be doing to Martín? She longed for him. So near, yet so occupied with their problems, he seemed distant.

Impulsively, over her light nightgown she threw a lace *rebosa* and went down the hall to his room. As there was no answer to her light knock, she hesitantly opened the door, sat down softly on the edge of his bed and gently began to massage his naked back. Her light touch woke him for an almost bottomless sleep. Catalina felt guilty. In his room, uninvited, she was robbing him of badly needed sleep. He looked up and gave her a sleepy smile. She leaned down, kissed him softly, red curls caressing his face, one hand gently on his neck, the other on his waist. He couldn't move. Slowly he pulled her down to lie next to him, her head on the pillow, inches from his. He rolled over, partially covering her body with his, put both hands behind her head, then pulled her face toward his to kiss her brow and eyes.

Like ballet dancers they touched each other lightly, elegantly. Their kisses were hard, deep and many until Catalina put her hand softly on his cheek to push him briefly away. In an agony of longing, daring, their eyes challenged each other. Tenderly, he slipped both hands under her nightgown, fingers curved to fit her strong, slender back, thumbs in the hollows of her damp armpits. As he slid his hands downward, Catalina's eyes stared longingly into his. His thumbs caressed her breasts, her nipples rising to meet his tender touch. Then he explored her flanks and followed the swell of her hips until the balls of his thumbs glided over the silken magic between her legs. Catalina's body trembled. His mouth dry, Martín knew he should stop but didn't think he could, and knew she wouldn't help him.

As he leaned over to kiss her again, hands softly cupping her breasts, the incongruity of a pistol shot dissolved their passion. For a second they gave each other a baffled stare almost as if they were strangers.

CHAPTER 24

MUFFLED BY THICK ADOBE WALLS, the shot sounded as if it came from in front of the *zaguan*. A heavy crash against its thick mesquite gates followed and reverberated throughout the *hacienda*. Martín took the stairs down two at a time while pulling on his shirt. Catalina followed, throwing the *rebosa* over her shoulders. Moments later, struggling into her robe, Margarita appeared. Out of his room off the kitchen dashed Tranquilo, almost colliding with Martín. The two sprinted to the office.

Where he had left it, Martín's Winchester stood behind the door. He disliked having loaded arms about, but anticipating trouble he had earlier thumbed shells into the magazine. Now the loaded rifle reassured him as he quickly levered in a round. Waving the others back, Martín stepped out of the office door and down the *zaguan*. With infinite care he slid back the iron bolts securing the small door to the heavy gates. Noiselessly, he lifted the latch and cracked open the door. It swung steadily inward. Why became tragically obvious. Pizarra, brain shot, had his head and neck propped against the small door. The horse's body and legs were sprawled outward. In a blind rage Martín fired shot after shot into the darkness, then dashed out.

A step behind him, Catalina screamed, "You're crazy. That's exactly what they want."

Brown, crouched in the darkness inside the front wall,

smiled at how easy it had been to lure Martín into the open. He aimed and fired at the dimly lit figure as it ducked out the small door. Never before having heard Catalina raise her voice, Martín abruptly halted. Brown's shot missed, slamming into the door frame inches from his shoulder. That split second halt saved him. Quickly he slipped back behind the massive mesquite gates, hesitating only long enough to move Pizarra's head out onto the step. In fury, he slammed closed and bolted the small door. Though he could feel his heart still pound from the close call and anger at the senseless cruelty, once back in the office Martín partially recovered his composure.

Eyes glistening, fists clenched, with a choked voice he turned to Catalina. *"Mi compadre,* Pizarra, dead! My closest friend since I was a boy." Then, "How can I thank you enough for warning me! *Dios,* I was stupid!"

Again Martín toured every inch of the *hacienda,* this time with Tranquilo, making sure doors were bolted and the tough, three-inch-thick mesquite shutters on the ground floor were barred In the center of each an aperture, shaped like a Greek cross, enabled a rifleman to fire up or down, left or right. Even against a direct assault, the shutters and thick walls should be sufficient. Adobe could absorb any bullet made, and the thick mesquite could stop or deflect all but close-up hits. Most vulnerable was the bedroom area on the second floor. Added after the last Navajo raiders had been shipped off to Bosque Redondo, no thought had been given to defense when the bedrooms were added. Their windows were covered with light louvered shutters to let in the river breeze and keep out the afternoon sun. Windows on the other side of the bedroom cross-hall looked onto the patio and were also covered with louvered shutters. They opened onto the roof of the *portal* that covered that end of the patio. As the *portal* was above twelve feet above the patio floor, he decided not to worry about them.

Even for a long siege they were prepared. Drinking water in clay *ollas* was stored in the kitchen, along with food for days. In case of fire, leather buckets full of water were placed strategically throughout the *hacienda*. Then Martín realized that only he was armed. A stupid oversight! Shotguns, pistols, rifles of various calibers were chained in a case behind the desk in Otero's office. Shells were sure to be locked in the drawer below the case. A quick rummage in the old Victorian desk produced keys for both the arms case and drawer.

"Take your pick, Tranquilo."

Villareal chose a Winchester rifle and Colt revolver, both chambered for the .44-.40 center-fire cartridge. One shell fit both pieces. Martín would not give up his rifle, and though he did not like it, reluctantly jammed in his belt Otero's favorite, a Colt .45 single-action pistol. In different pockets went cartridges for each weapon.

Over-prepared? Maybe. Yet more trouble seemed certain. The whole night was ahead of them. Midnight slipped by quietly. Martín fidgeted as he sat in the dark office. An hour or two later he saw through the cut-out in the shutter a glow to the south. Then flames and showers of sparks soared skyward. The barn, maybe even the corral, were in flames. He could do nothing but be thankful Pizarra had been shot, not burned to death. The women had to know. With slumped shoulders they took turns at the peephole to watch the decades-old structures burn exuberantly. The landscape was lighted from road to river.

With unexpected ferocity came the expected rain. In torrents and sheets it poured, harder, longer than any rain the Oteros could remember. The drains, not designed for such a downpour, clogged with accumulated debris, backed up and pooled water everywhere. In the patio it was inches deep, pouring over doorsills into the halls, flowing down them unchecked, into the office, even flooding the *sala* and *comedor*. For an hour the roar of rain on the flat roof of the *hacienda* and the tile-roofed *portal* drowned out all conversation. It was grimly satisfying watching the flames at the barn diminish, then disappear.

As the rain began to let up, with a hollow laugh Martín said, "I'll bet Brown is furious!"

Barn and corral could be rebuilt. His concern was for those who might have tried to save the stock and put out the fire. But he had heard no shots. Now was the time to do something positive. What made sense?

Tranquilo said, "It seems senseless just to sit here waiting for something else to happen."

Martín agreed. "What else can we do?"

"I'll go get the sheriff," he said.

"That's insane. You'll never make it."

"In the dark and rain it'll be easy to run from the kitchen door to the bosque down by the river. The grass is high. No one will see me. Down the river to the rope ferry is not much more than a mile. You've got to stay here with the señora and señorita. I'll be back before dawn with the sheriff."

Reluctantly, Martín realized his plan made sense. How many men did Brown have out there? He and Tranquilo were their obvious targets. Certainly not the women. But suppose accidentally —? He couldn't consider that possibility.

"Go get the sheriff," he said.

To cover Tranquilo's start to the river, he lay on the kitchen floor, Winchester at the ready. Reaching up, he cracked open the heavy door. Outside, clearing skies and multiplying stars shed enough light to see the *bosque* by the river. It looked anything but promising for Villareal's attempt, but he insisted on going. Noiselessly he slipped out the door, crouched and disappeared into the wet dark. For several heartbeats nothing happened. Relieved, Martín was about to close the door.

Conical muzzle flashes plumed from several rifles firing from the left to the right. Two dozen strides from the kitchen door Tranquilo rose from the deep grass only to crumple a step later. Martín angrily emptied his Winchester into the area from which the muzzle flashes had come.

Bolting the kitchen door, without a word he sprinted down the hall past the women crouching there. From the gun rack in the office he tore a double-barreled, twelve-gauge shotgun. In the drawer underneath the rack he found the killing shells he wanted, double "O" buck in brass casings. As he loped back to the kitchen, he broke open the breech of the shotgun and chambered two shells. He unlocked and flung the kitchen door wide open. Into the blackness Martín threw himself, coming to his feet in a crouch after rolling over several times. Both barrels of the shotgun spewed their deadly contents into the general area he had seen the muzzle flashes. Still in a crouch he ran a zig-zag pattern to where he figured Tranquilo had fallen. On the run he broke open the breech again to thumb in two more shells. He had guessed right, almost tripping over Tranquilo's body. Not a shot was fired as he dragged the limp mayordomo back in through the kitchen door. His shotgun seemed to have discouraged the competition.

Catalina, who had followed Martín into the kitchen, slammed and bolted the door behind him. By lantern light they examined Tranquilo, alive but unconscious. One bullet had penetrated his left cheek, exiting his mouth without touching his teeth. Another had pierced the calves of both legs. Expertly, Catalina washed and bandaged the three wounds. With doña Margarita's help she carried the mayordomo to the relative safety of the north hall running between the kitchen and parlor.

CHAPTER 25

TO CONCEAL WEARINESS and concern, Martín brusquely ordered the women, "Get dressed. It's going to be a long night."

Only two o'clock in the morning and Villareal was no longer able to help. As Margarita and Catalina left the office to change, he pounded on Manuel's desk in frustration and dropped his head onto his hands. Passive waiting maddened him. Initiative and action were his style.

Catalina heard the pounding, turned and re-entered the office to massage his slumping shoulders. "We're through the worst, I just know. It'll be morning soon and all this'll be over."

How naive, he thought, but didn't say it. Complimenting Catalina on her courage and optimism, secretly wishing he could share it, he said, "Your massage feels wonderful. Wish you didn't have to stop," and smiled at her as she left to dress.

Not only trapped by circumstances, but also literally trapped in the *hacienda*. Would his life continue to be made up of events he didn't want, could not control? Ralliere is right, he thought. This *is a* brutal land, but he had no choice but to live in it.

The priest had said, "Shoot only to wound if you have to shoot at all."

Easy to say, good Father, hard in reality.

Dawn was three and a half hours away. Brown and his people had plenty of time to force Martín to make another mistake or give up. What could he do all by himself? Here he was caged by the walls of the *hacienda*, no one to help him, hardly able to see to shoot. It could be worse. The building was like a fortress with impenetrable walls, heavy shutters. Otero's ancestors would never have anticipated its use for something like this. Fortunately, arms were plentiful, as were shells to match. Enough food and water had been laid in to last for days.

When the women returned to the office after dressing, Martín again barked out orders.

"Put out every lamp but that one on the floor behind the desk. I've got to be able to see in the dark. Lay down in the north hall near Tranquilo. You'll be safe there."

Well, relatively safe, he thought. Reluctantly, they left.

To disguise the fact that he was stalling, he spoke as if he knew what he was doing. What else could he do but react to whatever was done to them? Damn Whitney! He started all this. Alone in the office, Martín stared at the three shuttered windows, recalling his first visit when he waited nervously for Otero to appear.

Here he was again, nervous and waiting, certain that this time Brown would go for the *hacienda*. But where? The south and east office windows seemed most likely. He guessed they would use the third window, looking onto the patio, only if they had already broken into the *hacienda*. Why force an entry into the office? Brown, who'd been in it when he visited doña Margarita, would guess correctly that this was probably where he'd be and try to trap him.

He remembered how easily the real estate man had been boosted onto the roof of the *portal* surrounding the inner patio. Brown had seen it, too. His men could do the same. Those back bedrooms were vulnerable. So was the cross hall that ran in front of them, its thin shutters easily accessible from the *portal* roof and Brown smart enough to see it as a simple way into the *hacienda*.

On a hunch, Martín crossed over to the heavy mesquite shutter on the west window and through its cross-shaped peephole looked directly onto the patio. Starlight made the *portal* roofs quite visible. No sooner had he looked when the head and shoulders of a man appeared rising quickly, apparently boosted, until the man climbed onto the south *portal*. In stocking feet the intruder worked his way carefully down the sloping, still-wet tiles. At their edge he stopped and looked at the long drop to the flagstone surface. He hesitated, not wanting to be trapped on the patio.

Martín watched and waited. The man backed away from the edge toward what he was looking for, the flimsy shutters above the west *portal* roof. With a belt knife he pried one open. Quietly Martín slipped his rifle through the cross cut-out in the shutter and fired one shot, all he needed. Flattened by a shot between his neck and shoulder, with arms splayed up and out, his body accelerated feet first down the wet tiles, breaking several as it went over the edge. He dropped heavily, feet first, to the paving and, knees buckling, fell over backwards. Face up, he moved spasmodically. Brown wouldn't send anyone to try that way again.

At the sound of the shot, the women left Tranquilo and, at a run, crossed the *zaguan* through the parlor door and into the office.

"What was that shot? You all right?" asked Catalina, looking anxiously at Martín.

He lied. "I stupidly shot at a shadow. Now, for God's sake please stay in the other hall with Tranquilo. He needs you more than I do. And lock the parlor door into the *zaguan!*"

They re-crossed the *zaguan*.

Martín knew he had spoken too harshly. In a softer voice he called after them, "I'm sure all this will be over soon."

Just as he spoke, a hollow booming echoed down the empty *zaguan*. Its tough gates and small door, stiffened with oversize iron hinges, thick crossbars and massive bolts, held against whatever was being used as a battering ram. The attackers gave up.

Now where, wondered Martín, shuddering at the thought of the potential disaster the night might bring. The office still seemed a likely place to try and force an entry. Was he guessing right? Why not the parlor? Then he decided. Leaving the office door open, he positioned himself about ten feet down the hall, but where he could still see both of the office's shuttered windows. If Brown's men broke through the south or east window, they would be easy targets lighted by the dim glow of the kerosene lamp on the floor. He would be virtually invisible. He knelt down in the airless wet hall still flooded with rainwater. Over the years its adobe walls had dusted through their coating of *yeso*. Rainwater and the dust turned the hall into a slippery runway. One knee was in the film of mud on the tile floor. On the other Martín rested his elbows and rifle.

Minutes plodded by like hours. Maybe he was wrong about what Brown would do next. The thick adobe walls muffled all outside sound. His heart was racing, lungs pumping like bellows. Neither would help his aim. Air in the buttoned-up *hacienda* became even more oppressive. Sweat from Martín's armpits ran down his sides and the inside of his arms. Hands slippery from repeatedly mopping rivulets from his face and eyes made it difficult to hold his rifle or see clearly. His legs were cramping. When he could stand the ache no longer, he cautiously shifted his weight to put the other knee on the floor. It helped, barely. One more time he asked himself if Brown would try to force his way into the office.

A massive blow against the south side shutters of the office dispelled any doubt. After repeated ramming, the shutters bowed but did not break. With the fourth blow the iron pintles anchoring the hinged side of the heavy shutters began to give away, relinquishing their ancient hold deep in the adobe wall. At the fifth, both shutters burst inward, flinging the crossbar halfway across the room, followed closely by the post used as a battering ram.

Through the window a fusillade of shots from rifles, pistols and a shotgun ripped the room and its contents. Bookcases, the elegant mahogany gun rack, Victorian desk, chairs, horsehair-covered sofa, pictures, kerosene sconces on the wall, all were riddled and shredded. Walls, pocked with the impact of various missiles, showed brown through the white yeso. Yet still intact, casting a soft light on battered walls, was the kerosene lantern on the floor in the corner.

Silence. Martín knew but dreaded what would happen next. He silently wiped each hand on his pants and kept a ready eye on the office window, its shutters hanging crazily from their pintles. A gloved left hand slid carefully over the sill, followed by the head and shoulders of a man pulling himself into the room. In his right hand was a pistol. It was too easy. Would a shot to kill or just to wound be more likely to guarantee their safety? He close the latter.

When the man was too far into the room to retreat easily, Martín called out softly, "Move in any direction and you're dead."

The gunman whipped up his gun. Martín's shot broke the man's left elbow. In agony the man dropped his weapon to grab his arm, howled in pain and did a slow motion somersault into the room, ending up on his back. Catlike, already on the move, Martín grabbed and dragged the gunman into the hall. With a foot on his neck, Martin slipped off the man's belt and bound both hands firmly behind his back, then left him. Silence fell on the beleaguered *hacienda*. Where now?

Through the shattered window came a muffled, angry voice. "Goddamit, Brown, you said this was going to be easy. Nothin' about a gunman inside. Two hombres have already disappeared. Probably dead. We ain't no closer to inside than when we met you."

Martín visualized Brown's panic and smiled. Brown hardly needed a rebellion now. He snapped back, "All right! Finish the job and I'll raise the payoff to five double eagles."

"How about them other two?"

"They're no friends of yours. What they got coming I'll split with the rest of you."

That seemed to rekindle the mercenaries' enthusiasm. Unable to hear them leave, Martín waited in the hall to see what they would do next.

Believing the mayordomo had been killed or badly wounded, Brown reasoned an assault on the heavily shuttered windows of the parlor would be unopposed. Again came the sound of battering, this time from the parlor. Martín flung open the office door to cross the *zaguan*. He had forgotten that the south door to the parlor was locked and barred. Even his shoulder could not budget it. Desperate, he re-crossed the passageway at a run, dashed up the office hall, turned right past the *sala* and *comedor*, then down the far corridor toward the parlor cursing, "Goddamn this crazy house design!"

The Oteros lay face down in the hall, all but invisible in the dark, hands covering their heads. The pounding on the shutters continued. Catalina looked up pleadingly, her face a pale oval. Margarita sobbed.

Under repeated battering, the shutters finally gave. In the dim light Martín tried to draw a bead on the head and hands outlined in the shattered window opening. He pulled the trigger and the hammer simply clicked. He suddenly realized that in his haste he hadn't levered a fresh shell into the chamber of his rifle. He worked the lever frantically. The new round jammed in the receiver. The man in the window fired at Martín the near dark, the slug ricocheting against the adobe walls and burying itself in the door to the *sala*. No lantern on the floor to help his aim this time as he frantically fought to clear the jammed rifle. Catalina screamed. Martín was too late. He watched as from across the parlor the blast of a shotgun turned the intruder's face and chest to crimson. The man was literally blown back out the window.

Sitting propped against the parlor wall, the lower part of his face swathed in bandages, pants ripped to permit bandaging of his legs, smoke still trickling from the barrels of the shotgun across his lap, Tranquilo massaged his right shoulder. He looked up proudly as the surprised Martín stumbled into the room.

"Next best thing to a trip to the sheriff, eh, señor Martín? Why didn't you tell me not to fire this shotgun both barrels at once?"

Another volley of shots, but these from a distance and different direction. No bullet slapped against the adobe walls. A ragged answering salvo came from outside the demolished window. Still no sound of impact. Crawling to the opening, he peered over the torn body of the dead gunman. Only then did he realize it was early dawn. By its minimum light he saw four men, Brown and three others, backing down the space between the *hacienda* and its north flanking wall. Six well-armed men led by the grim sheriff, tall, stout John Bartlett, stalked through the front gate.

Martín turned around to look at Tranquilo. "You must have been wishing hard. You got the sheriff here."

Camp Brown knew he was through. So did his mercenaries. Without urging, all dropped the rifles and gunbelts. Raised hands seemed superfluous as they moved toward the armed sheriff and his deputies. While they passed the remains of the window, Martín made certain Brown and his men saw his cocked rifle. Over the bloody sill he climbed and followed them to the front gate.

Still game, Brown made one last try. Once out the front gate, he bolted for the nearest horse but never made it. An alert deputy clubbed him senseless with his rifle butt as Brown tried to climb into a saddle. Little time was wasted manacling the remaining gunmen and a very groggy Brown. Five deputies escorted them off to the jail in Belen. The sixth stayed with the sheriff.

When he saw Martín kneeling next to Pizarra lying in front of the *zaguan,* Bartlett extended his hand in genuine sympathy.

"That's a goddamned unnecessary shame. The man who did it ought to be shot in the head, too, or hung!"

"Maybe he will be," replied Martín.

Bartlett mustered a hint of a smile. "By God, Martín, you seem to attract trouble like molasses brings ants. Saw the fire way over in Belen. Wasn't sure it was La Constancia 'til one of your hands crossed the river and rustled me up. Said he figured you all were bottled up in the house.

"Some of the more adventurous types in town volunteered to come with me, so I deputized 'em and here we are. Now what the hell's been going on?"

Exhausted from the strain and emotion, Martín answered laconically, "Tried to burn us, then pry us out. Was about down to my last idea when you showed up."

"Damn if you didn't make it easy for us again!"

"Tranquilo finished it off. When they saw their friend go down at that parlor window, I suspect they began to doubt there'd ever be a payday. All we could really think about was holding out 'til it was light enough to see. Tranquilo's our only casualty, thank God!"

"I see the rest of the one Tranquilo nailed. Anybody else?"

"One tried to get in a second-floor window from the *portal* roof. He's lying in the patio not going anywhere, I believe. Another's tied up in the hall outside Otero's old office. Camp Brown, the hombre your man clubbed, used to work for Tom Catron in Santa Fe. Brown was the one who hired those birds. In Albuquerque, I suspect."

Martín's knees began to shake from fatigue and relief. "Sorry, sheriff, I've got to sit down."

Ready to crumple, he put his back against the front adobe wall, slid down it and wrapped his arms over his knees. The small door at the entrance to the *zaguan* cracked open, then swung fully wide. Relief shone on her face as Catalina ran to Martín, dropped to her knees, buried her head in his shoulder and wept.

Usually reserved, doña Margarita walked out and held the sheriff by the waist with both hands, and in a choked voice thanked him profusely. Bartlett purpled in embarrassment.

"You got the wrong man, señora," nodding in the direction of Martín. "All we did was tidy up a bit."

Lashed across a horse was the bloody body from in front of the parlor window. The other two gunmen were too injured to ride.

"Hate to ask you, Martín. Could you rustle up a wagon? Don't really care if these hombres live or die, but nobody's goin' to say I didn't treat 'em right."

CHAPTER 26

THE OFFICE was totally wrecked, a shambles. The only thing undamaged was the lantern on the floor. Martín blew it out and threw open the undamaged shutters. As distressed by the chaos as he knew the women would be, he could only stand in front of the damaged window to hide bloodstains of the man he shot in the elbow. Dazed, Catalina and her mother entered and looked around the office, wondering where to start bringing some kind of order back to it.

The night had been a mixed victory. But here in the devastation of Otero's office, Martín felt compelled to say, "Well, I guess we've won the battle, but unless we find those grants, we may lose the war."

Their search a failure so far, the women had to acknowledge that Martín was distressingly right. Catalina picked up a framed picture riddled by buckshot and shook off small flakes of *yeso*. With a grimace she re-hung it where it had been. Then she tried to right a brass sconce clinging drunkenly to the wall, its base almost bent double by a bullet.

"Do that again," said Martín abruptly.

"Do what again?" answered the startled Catalina.

"Swing that wall fixture up the way you did a moment ago."

Perplexed, she did as he asked, then stared at him.

Martín picked his way across through the room's debris and almost rudely shoved her aside to get at the fixture. Its base, once a handsomely stamped escutcheon, had been tortured into a useless shape by a bullet. Without a word he jerked the whole fixture off the wall. Both women looked at him as if he were insane.

Holding the sconce to one side, he peered at where it had been attached to the wall. A brass tube about an inch and a half in diameter and to which the sconce had been affixed was snugly inserted into the adobe wall. From across the room it had appeared to the practical Martín a complicated and expensive way to mount a relatively simple wall sconce. Now he knew there was more involved. Working it loose and withdrawing it using both index fingers, the tube came out stubbornly. He shook it and out slipped a slim roll of papers tied with a faded blue ribbon. Martín could not bear to even look at the roll. He handed it to Catalina without a word. All three inhaled and held their breaths as she slipped off the ribbon and flattened the papers out on the damaged desk. Margarita hung over one of her shoulders, he the other.

The roll consisted of two pieces of paper. Not only a copy of the original grant of La Constancia from the Spanish Crown, but also of its reconfirmation by the Untied States government. Wide-eyed in disbelief, Catalina looked first at Martín, then her mother.

"En el nombre de Dios!" she whispered as she sank to the floor in hysterical laughter mixed with tears.

Doña Margarita picked up the papers which had recurled and fallen when Catalina collapsed, looked at them again, then put both hands on Martín's cheeks and kissed him on the mouth. Astounded, embarrassed, he picked Catalina off the floor and kissed her hard.

With a wry smile he turned to the two women and said, "Don't you think it'd be nice to send a thank-you note to Camp Brown?"

EPILOGUE

ALTHOUGH THIS STORY combines real and fictional characters, there is nothing fictional about the Estancia Valley's grim history in the mid 1880s, the period in which the narrative is set.

Much of the conflict then was over land and water, a contest between descendants of the early Hispanic settlers and the more recently arrived Anglo-Americans. Conflicts over land and water exist today and are still the main issues that divide people of Hispanic descent and "Anglos."

Surprisingly, GRINGO & GREASER was the actual and provocative name of the newspaper which began publication in 1883 by the idiosyncratic Charles Kusz, a liberal immigrant from New York state. Its readership was primarily in the racially charged atmosphere of the Estancia Valley. GRINGO & GREASER's pro-Hispanic content, astounding for that period, was as uncompromising as its name.

Kusz was assassinated in 1884, probably to no one's surprise considering the editorial content of his newspaper. His killer was never found. Presumably Kusz also knew who was behind local cattle rustling, a major valley industry. That knowledge and the tone of GRINGO & GREASER were no doubt reasons for his death.

After the shoot-out at Manuel Otero's Estancia Springs ranch, badly wounded James Whitney, the impulsive egotist who started it, survived a long and painful trip by wagon and reached the just-completed St. Vincent's Hospital in Santa Fe. There he was kept alive by a dedicated nurse, a nun of Mexican parentage named Sister Maria Teresa. She was Manuel Otero's sister. Aware of and despite the fact that Whitney had killed her brother, she felt it her Christian duty to do everything possible to save his life.

Just before the Santa Fe sheriff arrived with a warrant for his arrest, Whitney was spirited out of the hospital by his brother Joel and others who lowered him from a window. Later arrested, then released on a sizable bond posted by Joel, James Whitney was finally tried in April of 1884. In the words of a contemporary news account, Whitney was acquitted "by the best jury money could buy." In twelve months he was dead of the wounds inflicted by Ernesto Henriquez, Otero's brother-in-law.

The fatal gun battle that killed Manuel B. Otero at his Estancia Springs ranch need never have happened. The land in dispute between Otero and Whitney was over the Baca Grant, claimed by both. Half of it was overlapped by land bought by a man named Gervacio Nolan. Several years before selling that land to James Whitney and his brother Joel, Nolan had offered it to the Oteros for the bargain sum of $5,000. Otero's attorneys advised him that Nolan's deed to the land was worthless. Had the Oteros ignored their advice, there would have been no sale to the Whitneys, no illegal takeover by them of Estancia Springs, and no killings. Indeed, the Oteros' claim to the grant might never have been challenged.

As it happened, the legal contest between the heirs of Manuel Otero and the Whitneys dragged on for fourteen years until an appeal to the U.S. Supreme Court in 1898 led to a final decision. Unexpectedly, the Court ruled that neither party had a valid claim to either grant.

It is also of interest, but not a part of this novel, that Manuel Otero's nephew became governor of New Mexico Territory in the late 1890s.

After the Supreme Court decision, these vast tracts of

land were opened to homesteading. Farmers rushed in to stake claims. By the 1920s the valley had become known as the "pinto bean capitol of the world." To provide equipment and service to the farmers, the town of Estancia was established on the site of Otero's Estancia Springs Ranch. In the 1930s drought wiped out all farming activities in the valley.

Manzano, which had very little to recommend it one hundred and twenty years ago, has lost much of its population and what little commerce and tiny industry existed. But the legendary apple orchard that gave its name to the town still exists and even today bears shriveled fruit.

Quarai Mission, one of three great valley monuments to the faith and industriousness of seventeenth century Franciscans, has profited from the passage of years. Ceded to the Museum of New Mexico in 1913 by conscientious owners of its land, it became a state monument in 1935 and was transferred to the National Park Service in 1981. In each instance restoration and preservation has continued.

Father Jean Baptiste Ralliere of Tome served his parish and town for fifty-four years until his retirement in 1911.

In 1879 Manuel Otero's father, after recovering from a serious illness, donated a bronze bell to father Ralliere's Church of the Immaculate Conception. Almost twelve decades later the bell can be seen, still unused, in the grass outside the church. Unforgiving after their bitter feud over water, the priest had chiseled off from the shoulder of the bell the names of Otero and his wife.

Manuel Otero's former *estancia*, La Constancia, and its idyllic site on the Rio Grande is now a small town bearing the name "Constancia."

The End